GONE FISHING

To Mrs Edwards

Anzie H. Norris 2012

GONE FISHING

❀

A Novel of
Old Florida and Her Tragic Seas

Anzie Harris Norris
with Rusty Fischer

iUniverse, Inc.
New York Lincoln Shanghai

Gone Fishing
A Novel of Old Florida and Her Tragic Seas

Copyright © 2006 by anzie harris norris

iUniverse books may be ordered through booksellers or by contacting:

iUniverse
2021 Pine Lake Road, Suite 100
Lincoln, NE 68512
www.iuniverse.com
1-800-Authors (1-800-288-4677)

This is a work of fiction. All of the characters, names, incidents, organizations and dialogue in this novel are either the products of the author's imagination or are used fictitiously.

ISBN-13: 978-0-595-40182-6 (pbk)
ISBN-13: 978-0-595-84559-0 (ebk)
ISBN-10: 0-595-40182-1 (pbk)
ISBN-10: 0-595-84559-2 (ebk)

Printed in the United States of America

This book is dedicated in memory of those who survived this true-life disaster. May God bless them all for the remainder of their days...

Anzie Norris wishes to thank these special people in her pursuit to write this story. Dolores Jennings, widow of Fred, Homer Hooks, and Lois Cowles Harrison and Hollis Hooks, whom, without their encouragement, this would not have been possible. To my lovely daughters Anne, Betty Jo, Lynn and Krysta. Finally, to my wonderful friend Jayne, who said to me "let's type it up!" Thank you all from the bottom of my heart.

A special thanks to my Pastor, and his family, to all my special friends in the Searchers Sunday School Class for your help.

A very big thank you to Rusty Fischer/Freelancer. You were a big help. Also, to Martha Bouchee, and Wendy Harrison, you always listened.

To my grandchildren. You are so awesome. You are the best.

To Barbara Barfield, thanks for the change in direction.

I must, in all fairness, thank my brothers and sisters for listening to bits and pieces of this work for more than four years. I am so glad you are mine. I am lucky to have you in my life. Thank you again, your sis, Baganucchi...

To Oprah Winfrey. You are such an inspiration. You inspire us to dig deep and do things we only ever Dreamed of in our life time. I thank you from the bottom of my heart. You make us all strive to set higher standards for ourselves, to achieve the very best for our lives. Thank you so much!

Glossary

Mable Jennings—   Widow of Frank. They had six children, four girls and two boys. She works at Greens Drug Store lunch counter week days until 2pm.

Jennings girls—   Anne, married to Bobby they have five children and live in Madison FL

Sunny, married to Will. Will drives for a trucking company, Sunny is a homemaker—they have three children.

Wanda—married to Terry they live in nearby Homeland. Wanda is a Hair dresser, Terry pilots a glass bottom boat at Silver Springs, they have five children.

Ginny—married three years to Pete, they own Ocala Plumbing & Hardware and both work in the store. No children.

Fred Jennings—   Married to the lovely Dolores. She is expecting their first child in one month. He works as a telephone lineman. They declined the invitation to join the group charter.

Ed Jennings—   Youngest son, still in High School.

Passengers and Crew

Captain—   LB Wilson, married to Lauren, they have three children.

1st Mate—   Buck Gibbs he and his wife Betty Jo have three children.

Lex & Lacey Ross—   They own the Family Shoe Store and have three children.

Bill & Lois
Saunders—   Bill is a popular barber, he cuts the hair of the male passengers. Lois is a homemaker; they have three children.

Searchers—   Sheriff John H Harris married to Noma, they have two boys.

                            Chief Deputy Mat McGuire married to Krysta, one daughter and two boys.

                            Mayor John Marshall Green

                            People of Ocala, Yankeetown and Cedar Key

Sam Pettus &
Annalee Morgan—   Sam is in college, Annalee works at Silver Springs greeting visitors throughout the park. They were recently "pinned".

Hank & Kate Mays— He works at Caviness New Car dealership, she works at Saunders Real Estate.

CHAPTER 1

Shave and a Haircut

It was late June 1948 and the Noon hour came in hot to Ocala, a quaint little town smack dab in the center of Central Florida. With the lazy summer workday officially half over, much might have been said, but little was most likely done. (Unless, that is, you could count socializing on your time card.)

But then, that's the way the locals like it. After all, life moved slow here, and with good reason. Some blamed the heat, which in the middle of summer could sap the life out of a newborn, others blamed the humidity, which could make a man's shirt sleeves stick to his forearms, and that was just on the *way* to work.

At the end of the day, though, most just cherished the lifestyle that such sleepy little towns provider the happy, peaceful residents. Life in Ocala, much like the city's name, was short and sweet.

As in many such small, southern towns, the some 6,000 residents of Ocala knew each other not just by name or by face, but by living rooms and wrap-around porches and Sunday church services and ice cream socials and afternoon glasses of lemonade shared on wooden rockers and cooled by the breeze of hand-held fans.

Here the druggist knew what day you'd be coming in for your medicine, the seamstress knew to let out your dresses after gaining a few pounds during the holidays and to take them back in as you prepared for summer strolls on the beach, and the pastor knew whether or not you'd be coming to church on Sunday by how you walked—or staggered—home come Saturday night.

Here life oozed along like the rays of the sun, languid, steamy, and bitter-sweet. You were more likely to run across a gator than a stranger, and news from the outside world was far less important than the local grapevine, which was heavy on gossip and short on politics.

Unless, of course, the two crossed paths, as they were often wont to do…

Families lived in tight-knit neighborhoods of open doors and covered dishes and neighbors weren't just neighbors, they were friends. Doors stayed unlocked, windows stayed open, and porches weren't just for potted plants and swinging chairs, they were a second living room.

This fin Ocala day was like all the others; hot, humid, sunny, lazy, familiar, and friendly. Around the bustling downtown area, a wide main street lay bordered with several family run businesses that had been standing since the turn of the century.

Here bicycles were as common as cars, though Ocala's male folk did pride themselves on owning the latest and greatest automobiles the local dealerships had to offer. (Even if most of them had to wait a few years before they could afford them—the 1949's had just come out!)

As noon approached, one of Ocala's most popular businessmen, Pete Peterson, stared at the empty aisles of the Ocala Hardware Store and checked his watch for the ninth time in as many minutes.

It was a little early for lunch, but if he waited too much longer some customer might wander in and begin asking questions about this weight nail or that size screw, and then before you it he'd be late!

Instead, he walked to the windowed front door and hung his well-used "Gone to Lunch" sign where it would be the most prominent. Before shutting the door behind him, Pete sighed contentedly.

Here was his world, a universe that was heavy on sawdust and roof beams and porcelain and pipes. He knew drains, faucets, and sinks like he knew his own hands.

Pete was slim and trim with black curly hair. He dressed casually for work; you never knew when you'd have to take a call personally, but cleanly. His cobalt blue eyes were warm and friendly, and many was the customer who frequented Pete's store for less of his hammers and nails and more of his smiles and good-natured ribbing.

At only 29, Pete was half-owner of the town's hardware store with his wife, Virginia, or "Ginny," as he called her. A 25-year-old, raven-haired beauty, Ginny was the light in Pete's eye, and the fact that they'd been married for three blissful years without kids had less to say about their desire to bear children than it did about their desire to enjoy "what was left of their honeymoon."

A honeymoon most friends felt they were still on…

Ginny had left a few minutes earlier to meet her friends for lunch, and he had smiled to see her jaunty summer hat disappear around the corner as she sashayed her way to their favorite lunch spot.

Theirs was a good life, and many in town marveled at how the two could not only live and play together, but work together as well. Most men hurried to work each morning, if for no other reason than to flee the coop and be rid of the henpecking.

Most wives were glad to see them go!

But not Pete and Ginny. Though they often frequented the shop at different hours—Pete liked to kid that Ginny spent most of her days drumming up business in the beauty parlor—most of their day was spent replenishing stock together, taking service calls, and keeping the books.

It was the rare day that saw either of them stay home sick, and it wasn't just because they were running their own business. As much as they enjoyed the "working" part of working together, they were just as happy with the "together" part.

Pete and Ginny might have been local celebrities thanks to their thriving business, not to mention romance, but their family cherished them for quite a different reason: their pets!

Perhaps befitting their perpetual honeymoon, Pete and Ginny were the owners of two vibrantly colored lovebirds and Pete and Petey. (Though it was a closely guarded secret, these were the couple's "pet names' for each other in the privacy of their own home.)

Peach and green, the two lovebirds—those of the feathered variety, that is—could often be seen preening in their birdcage. When neighbors came to call or at family gatherings at the house, Ginny often hung the birdcage on a low branch so that all could enjoy the lovebirds' rare and colorful beauty.

Ginny's nieces and nephews, especially, loved to come visit their aunt and gaze endlessly at the preening pair, bedecked in all their feathered finery and basking in the sunshine as well as the company. These feathered lovebirds were almost as popular about town as Pete and Ginny themselves.

As Pete at last watched Ginny's hat disappear around the bend, he turned the key into his lock with a satisfying click and noticed only as he was walking away that the "Out to Lunch" was hanging rather crookedly.

Smiling to himself, he made a quick mental note to try and beat Ginny back to the store; she'd fuss at him for sure if she saw it hanging that way. A born perfectionist, Ginny had been known to send him back home to change his shirt if she'd discovered a stain there after lunch or, more often than not, coffee.

"Why, what will the customers think, Pete?" She was often heard to say as he ambled, chin down, shoulders low, for the quick trip back home to change. "This store isn't just a reflection of our business, honey; it's a reflection of us!"

"You wouldn't buy a car from someone who drove an old, broken down jalopy now, would you? So why should our customers buy pipes and plungers, hammers and nails from a messy slob?"

Pete was often heard to mumble as he made his way back home for a quick morning change, "If you saw some of the customers' plumbing I've used plungers on, Ginny, you'd let me come to work in grease-stained overalls and bare feet!"

Staring at the crooked sign, the practical joker in young Pete was just as eager to beat her back to the store after lunch, lurk around the corner by the shoe store, just behind the giant Brogan hanging from the store sign, and have a front row seat to her reaction. He shrugged contentedly, sauntering off to the local barber's with an extra special jaunt to his step.

Such was the midday entertainment in sunny Ocala, Florida…

As Pete sauntered down the street, he happened upon an old friend and frequent customer, Lex Ross. A local businessman like himself, Lex was just putting his own "Gone to Lunch" sign out on the door of his busy Family Shoe Store. (A tad enviously, Pete had to admit, Lex's sign was a much fancier affair than his own!)

Then again, with age comes experience: at 38-years-old, Lex was nearly a decade older than young Pete, and had been in business for most of his adult life. The name of Lex's store—Family Shoe Store—was symbolic of his happy life: Lex was married to a beautiful soul named Lacey, and together they had three gorgeous children, ranging in age from the two girls, who were 12 and 10, and their only boy, a 7-year-old.

Family was everything to Lex, and he saw in his young friend Pete a kindred soul. Together the two greeted each other with a warm handshake and the news of the day, as they walked in step just a few feet down to their mutual destination: the Arcade Barber Shop.

But the Arcade, with its revolving red, white, and blue barber pole and five-year-old magazines scattered about the spacious waiting room, was more than just a place to get your hair cut or shoes shined; it was a meeting place for young and old, rich and poor, to come and gather and share what womenfolk called gossip, but men preferred to call "news."

The Arcade had been around for as long as anyone could remember, and the décor proved it. Proud newspaper clippings touting record fishing trips or tournament wins lined a bulletin board just outside the men's room. (There was no ladies' room.)

Posters for Berma-Shave and Goody's Powder served as decorations of a sort, though of course the current president held sway in a framed photo courtesy of good old Uncle Sam. Several beat-up chairs lined the huge plate glass window that fronted Main Street as customers and loiterers alike faced the three formal barber chairs that dominated the center of the sprawling storefront.

Behind each chair stood a cabinet heaped with straight razors and sharpened scissors. A tabletop radio played from one corner, quietly filling the air with pleasant background music.

Pete and Lex sauntered in, finding themselves just in time, as head barber, proprietor, and resident comedian Bill Saunders was just finishing telling a story to one of his customers.

Bill, a handsome man of 40 who's dark hair made him look years younger stood brandishing scissors in one hand and a comb in the other as he delayed finishing a haircut to finish his story instead.

With a baritone voice worthy of radio Bill continued, "An old man of 85 feared his wife was getting hard of hearing. So, one day he called her doctor to make an appointment to have her hearing checked. The doctor made an appointment for a hearing test in two weeks time, but in the meantime the husband was to give her what the doc called an 'informal test' so he could give the doctor an idea of the seriousness of the problem.

"So the doctor says, 'Here's what you do: start out about 40 feet away from her and, in a normal speaking voice, see if she hears you. If not, try asking her something from 30 feet, then 20 feet, and so on until she answers'

"Well, the old fellow took the doc's advice and, that very evening, the wife is in the kitchen cooking dinner and he is in the living room. He says to himself, 'I'm about 40 feet away, let's see what happens.' Then in a normal tone he asks, 'Honey, what's for supper?' No answer.

"So he moves a little closer to the dining room, about 30 feet away, and repeats his question: 'Honey, what's for supper?' Again the old fella gets no response. So he moves closer, until he's only about 20 feet away, and asks her the same question all over again. Nothing happens. So he walks up to the kitchen door, about 10 feet away, and says one last time, 'Honey, what's for supper?'

"So what does the old gal do? Well, she turns around and says, 'Darn it, Earl, for the fourth time: CHICKEN!'"

Bill chuckled at his own joke before saying, "Okay, Homer, that's the joke for the day. You can hop down and I'll take that," as he took the striped cloth from around Homer's neck, "I'll have a new joke next time."

"Thanks, Bill," his satisfied customer replied. "I'll look forward to it, same time in three weeks?"

"Sure," replied Bill, not even bothering to pencil it in on his oft-ignored calendar. He knows Homer and he knows his schedule. "11:30 Friday is good for me if it's good for you." With a friendly nod and a familiar handshake, the two men concluded their business together.

Bill's habits were as rigid as his stance; his customers knew when it was time to come and time to go. Glancing up at the clock, it was clearly time to go. And if the clock wasn't enough of a hint, Bill always made sure to cast off his bleach-white apron with a flourish, signifying lunchtime was indeed at hand.

Bill, sporting an anchor tattoo on his right forearm from his days spent in the Navy, was a family man just like Pete and Lex. Married for nearly fifteen years to his lovely wife, Lois, he boasted three children at home, none of whom wanted to be a barber!

It mattered little to Bill. Since buying his own shop more than a decade ago, the popular barber and respected businessman had done well for his family, and was hopeful that his brood would do even better for themselves.

As he ushered everyone out, Bill locked the door and put up his own "Gone to Lunch" sign. It was faded and yellow and made young Pete feel that much better about his own sign.

The three might have been an unlikely group, but for years now they had been having lunch together at the same time, same place. Bill joined his friends on the steamy sidewalk and together the three men strolled straight to Green's drugstore for lunch.

They weren't alone: inside the soda sop a group of young ladies also gathered for lunch, as they did several times a week. They sat at one of the five or six small, round tables dotting the black and white marble floor.

A lazy ceiling fan was slowly revolving overhead as the women eyed the daily lunch specials. Green's was typical of southern drugstores at the time, part store, part lunch counter, crowded, but typically low key and quiet nonetheless. From shoe polish to cough drops, from greeting cards to toenail clippers, you could get it at Green's.

If the Arcade was the local gathering spot for Ocala's male citizenry, then Green's was the same for its female contingent. Here they met, shopped, gossiped, and ate; often at the same time! Unlike the occasionally rowdy atmosphere where the boys hung out, however, Green's had a more subdued atmosphere.

Summer hats firmly affixed to their heads, the ladies who lunched, just as often strolled up one aisle of Green's and down the other, idly choosing various sundries which had drawn them in from the heat of Main Street.

Much like their shopping trips, lunchtime was a very casual, friendly affair, often stretching well past an hour if the gossip, or the lunch, was particularly good on any given day. Particularly on Fridays!

On this sunny Friday three longtime friends, Analee Morgan, Kate Mays, and Ginny Peterson sat at their favorite table, located halfway between the wide windows facing Main Street.

They greeted each other warmly and settled in for a leisurely repast of whatever homemade goodies Green's had to offer. They had plenty of time; all three women worked within two blocks of the soda shop, and the longer they lingered over their blue-plate specials, the quicker they hot-footed it back to work.

Perhaps the lunches were so friendly because they were so familiar. Ginny's mother, Mabel Jennings, single-handedly ran the lunch counter with a heart of gold. A kind, wise face perched on her small frame. Her popular counter served only lunch, a light fair of sandwiches, salads, sodas, and the like.

Mabel smiled at her son-in-law, Pete Peterson, as he found a table with his two cronies, Lex and Bill, and then saw to asking Ginny and her two friends what they were in the mood for.

There was no need for pen and paper when spry Mabel took an order. In the three years she'd been running Green's kitchen she'd yet to forget either an order, nor had she called in sick in all that time.

Luckily, Ginny and the gals were an easy table: fresh chicken salad, brimming with chunks of thinly sliced celery, for all three women, then only variation being their drink order. From a tray Mabel deposited two Cokes, one for her daughter and the other for Analee, and a glass of milk for Kate.

Mabel, cocking her eyebrow a the odd drink order, nonetheless wished the women a "great lunch" before rushing back to the counter to fill more lunch orders.

In her absence, Kate confessed to her girlfriends in a hushed voice that bore witness to the modesty of that bygone era: "Girls, I just know I'm, well, you know, in the family way." After the squeals and congratulations from her closest girlfriends, Kate added, "I've got an appointment with Dr. Meade on Monday to be sure, but until then I'm not sure."

Ginny, at the age of 24, longed for children of her own to hold. Her sister, Anne, had five precious little ones. She smiled at Kate and said, "We'll hold off on congratulating you just yet," as Ginny nodded in the direction of Hank, Kate's husband, who was sitting in the next booth, having just joined the rest of his regular foursome, Pete, Lex, and Bill.

The girls giggled admiringly, even as Kate blushed. They were right, of course: Kate had been lucky to find such a dashing, handsome husband in Hank Mays, a 31-year-old new car salesman who kept her riding in style and as excited about his nightly homecoming as he was about the new styles of cars that came out each year.

Hank and Kate were typical of most young couples in Ocala: vibrant, full of fun, and yet just as eager to put in a hard day's work to assure their future.

Analee, the only single gal at the table, was envious of both Ginny and Kate and, of course, their doting, handsome husbands. A tall girl with a bright smile and an even brighter mind, she was not married, but dating her boyfriend, a handsome young college student named Sam Pettus.

She and Sam had been dating only a few months, but already Analee was certain Sam was the man for her and that, if only he could be given a nudge in the right direction, he would surely "see the light."

For his part, Sam worried that he couldn't support her, and fretted constantly over finishing his degree in engineering at the nearby university. But Analee wasn't worried; they could live on love for the time being and, of course, her better than most salary from her job in a nearby office down at the Marion County Agriculture Department.

Analee knew it was silly to compete with her two best friends, but still she couldn't help feeling as if perhaps life was already getting by her. At 22, she was only two years younger than Kate, already happily married for several years and, now, expecting her first child with handsome Hank.

"Will I ever catch up?" Analee pondered aloud as her two friends dug into their overflowing chicken salads.

The two diners laughed before reassuring their lithe and leggy friend. "Don't be in such a rush," cautioned Ginny, although she'd never regretted marrying her man Pete for a second. "Look at you: smart, beautiful, independent, a real 'modern woman.' Pretty enough to be a cover girl, smart enough to write for whatever magazine would put you there, why, any man would be glad to have you for his bride."

"And if that young man Sam Pettus doesn't snap you up off the market jiffy quick, he might just find he's a day late and a dollar short. In the meantime, just enjoy yourself. Don't be so quick to rush into marriage and making babies."

"Amen!" said Kate, although she was hardly convincing as she winked openly at her husband in the next booth. "What I wouldn't give to be footloose and fancy free from time to time!"

"Listen to you," Analee parried with a laugh, finally digging into her mouth-watering salad. "I've never seen anyone happier to only suspect that they're pregnant, true or not!"

"She's right, Kate," joined in Ginny with a conspiratorial wink at her single friend. "You're already glowing, and it's not even a done deal!"

Kate couldn't argue with that, even as she sipped slowly at her milk and tried desperately to rearrange what remained of her salad so that Mabel wouldn't think she hadn't enjoyed what little of it she'd eaten.

Truth was, she'd been nauseous for weeks now, another sign, at least to her, that surely she must be with child. She was enjoying the day, the company, the meal, but inside her she yearned desperately to know the truth.

Looking at Hank munching on a ham sandwich only a booth away, she smiled to think of how he would take the news. All the girls in town had been so jealous when he'd chosen Kate to be the one who took him "off the market."

But behind the boyish smile, drop-dead gorgeous blue eyes and curly brown hair, Hank, the car salesman, brash, loud, and cocky was but his public persona. At home, whether sitting together in their living room or sharing their bed, he was loving and kind, sensitive to her fragile emotions and playful when her sometimes overanxious moods needed lightening.

Oh, he was a man's man, no doubt about it, but away from his buddies, he was a gentle lover, doting partner, and adoring husband. Though Kate considered herself plain, at least in comparison to the legions of busty blondes and raven-haired beauties who'd pursued Hank during heir high school years, the man she'd married made her feel like a princess night and day.

As lunch wound down, the almost strict segregation that had found the women sittin gat one table and the men at another eventually breaks down as the conversation shifts to talk of the big grouper-fishing trip planned for later that weekend.

Bill Saunders, the group comedian, engaged the women in conversation by teasing, "Ladies, come this weekend you'll be dining on fresh grouper by the plate full. I can reel in those fish as well as I can cut hair."

Analee, not having known Bill as long as the other girls, but well aware of his reputation as a great jokester and fisherman, chimed in with a quick, "Then I guess we better order some fish to go, right ladies? Otherwise we might starve come Sunday night."

Laughter rippled across both tables. As Bill bragged to Kate about "the one that got away," the conversation on the women's side grew lively as Ginny addressed Analee. "I'm so glad you and Sam can take the place of my brother, Fred, and his very pregnant wife, Dolores, on our fishing trip. She is due next month, you know, so not surprisingly they think it best to stay on dry land."

Analee replied conspiratorially, "We're only too happy to fill in for them, Ginny. I know Sam will enjoy the break and, truth be told, I'm no great fan of the open sea. I suppose I just want to be with Sam. Does that make me a horrible friend?"

Ginny laughed openly at her friend's honesty. "Not at all," she assured her. "Why, where do you think they got the saying 'too many fish in the sea' from in the first place?"

Bill Saunders joined in the conversation saying, "It's official. I finally talked to my wife, Lois, into going. She loves to fish, but is really afraid of deep water. She won't be happy very far from land. Most of the time I take her fishing from the bank. That's about as close to the water as I've gotten her so far. You know, she had a friend that drowned when they were just kids. It has made her scared of being in the water ever since."

In a rare moment of refreshing honesty the man known mostly for his ribald jokes and unceasingly positive exterior went on to say, "Lois spends all her time with our kids. I want her to relax and have some fun. This weekend her mom is coming for a visit. Her mom is so great with the children that this time, Lois can't say no. I can't wait. I just know we'll all have a great time."

Bill's eyes looked momentarily sad in the wake of his confession, as if perhaps he was only trying too hard to convince himself. The girls knew it was a major step for his wife, Lois, to agree to the trip, and that it would be an uphill battle for the couple until the very minute the boat left the dock.

As the men shifted focus by talking about the new 1949 Oldsmobile that had just come out the week before, Ginny Peterson tried to lighten the mood by adding, "My sister, Anne, and her family are coming tomorrow. We are having a family picnic so I need to go talk to Momma."

She walked over to the still busy counter and signaled to her Mom. When Mabel came over, she smiled as Ginny said, "Momma, I'm going soon. Thanks for lunch, it was amazing as always. Listen, I'll call you later to see what I need to bring to the picnic."

Mabel answered with a beaming smile, "Okay, I can't wait to see how all the grandkids have grown."

As she turned back to her work, she grinned to watch Ginny walk back and take Pete's hand for the short walk back to the store. *Those two*, she thought to herself, *what a couple of lovebirds...*

CHAPTER 2

Family Picnic

Mabel Jennings was a widow; a petite lady with short hair and a long la a group of admirers, among whom she was proud to list family and friends. Her husband, Frank, had passed away four years previously from heart disease, leaving her the old, rambling house and six beautiful children, four girls and two boys.

The years after Frank's death had been hard on Mabel and the kids, but the warm people of Ocala and her large family had boosted her spirits and given her the reason to go on.

She'd since made peace with the loss; though there wasn't a day that went by that she didn't turn around a dozen times, expecting to see Frank staring back at her each time.

Now her children and their families kept her busy enough. After spending the week running the small lunch counter inside Green's drug store, the diminutive lady enjoyed being home.

With all four of her daughters flown from the nest, not to mention three with children of their own, Mabel had but one son left at home: Ed, a teenager, who despite his good nature, or perhaps because of it, kept her as busy as the four girls had with various church activities, dates, and other social occasions. Her other son, Fred, who was married to Dolores, would also be at the picnic. They were expecting a baby in one month.

Mabel's house was as tidy as her lunch counter with a place for everything and everything in its place. Mabel normally enjoyed the solitude of her weekends. Typically, Ed was off exploring their 30 acres. He was a popular boy, and stayed busy and busy often meant gone. With his gangly-limbs, voracious appetite, and winning smile gone from the house, Mabel could regain control of her typical Florida one-story home, complete with screened porch in front and in back and shade trees everywhere.

She walked from room to room, dusting here or plumping up a throw pillow there. She was an ardent lover of plants, as witnessed by the ample garden just beyond her back door and the potted plants that dotted every windowsill in her four-bedroom house. Frank had added on rooms as needed. She addressed each plant personally, though she was not eccentric enough to name them, and yet treated them as lovingly and passionately as she had her own children. With a "There, there now" or an "Isn't that nice?" she swept from room to room, checking on her "babies."

This Saturday, in particular, found her busier than ever as she prepared for the passel of guests that would soon be invading her normally tranquil home. Happily invading, she was quick to add as she put the finishing touches on her spotless kitchen and well-ordered living room.

She had spent the morning in her own kitchen, ready for the onslaught of casseroles, salads, and desserts that would soon be arriving in the arms of her girls, and making room in her icebox and clearing every available inch of counter space. Now she rested comfortably on her screened porch, several wooden rockers lined up informally alongside a porch swing. She had a glass of lemonade in one hand and a fan in the other, awaiting the first of her guests to arrive.

It was the pleasant calm before the long-awaited storm, a moment of tranquility and relief sandwiched between a busy morning and what was sure to be an even more hectic afternoon. Still, Mabel loved these moments of family togetherness, which were becoming more and more rare these days.

When the girls had first married, it had been easier for all of them to get together. For the most part her four beautiful girls had been wooed by local boys. Now her family was spread out a little further, and even before the babies were born, she had felt a pulling at her apron strings, a longing to be free. Her daughters were wives and mothers, with lives and families of their own. They lived only miles away; Wanda was only 17 miles away, and Anne, the furthest, now lived in Madison, which was over 100 miles away. Mabel was far from lonely. Her daughters called frequently and sent cards and baby pictures, and for that she was grateful. They were good, dutiful, family-oriented daughters, and she had no reason to blame them for doing what they'd been taught!

So the family picnic set for that afternoon was a rare luxury and she intended to enjoy every minute of it. They'd started the annual tradition years back, once the babies were old enough to travel and the older kids behaved enough to help look after them.

Summer was the perfect time for a reunion, as Mabel rarely saw Anne between the special holiday of Easter and the summer holidays. This way she could have something to look forward to after the egg hunts and pretty bonnets, and before the watermelons were cut and firecrackers were lit on the 4th of July.

Mabel sighed with contentment, pleased at the family she'd raised, and felt a twinge of regret that her late husband wasn't here to see his own hand in the girls' maturity.

"How Frank would have loved a day like today," she thought as she took an extra long swallow of the lemonade before setting it down on the nearest end table. She gazed across the wide expanse of her green front lawn, eyeing the barbecue grill freshly filled with kindling wood and awaiting only the hamburgers and hot dogs she had stacked high on multi-colored platters in the icebox.

She noted the old bedspreads and sheets scattered around the ground. Held down at each corner with rocks from her garden and looking expectantly as they awaited a gathering of kids to enjoy their smooth, soft comfort. There were also two swings in the yard, big enough to seat two comfortably. She craned her neck to see the checkerboards and jump ropes and jacks arranged neatly at on end of the porch, where the smaller children loved to play together and whisper and laugh and frolic as the adults did the same, never farther than a watchful eye away.

Only when the distant sound of an approaching car reached her ears did Mabel interrupt her pleasant reverie to spot the familiar faces of her daughter, Sunny, and her husband, Will, smiling to beat the band as they made their way up her gravel drive. Their three children, Betty Jean, who was fourteen, and their two boys, Tony and Jason, ages nine and three, crowded in the backseat fighting for purchase between their parents' shoulders and eager to be the first to wave to "Gramma."

Mabel breathed a sigh of relief to see the smiling family, and waited patiently on her shady porch as Will parked his car into a corner of the yard. She marveled at the love her daughter and her husband shared. It reminded her so of her love for Frank. Now married for nearly two decades, Sunny and Will were the very picture of love and devotion. It always made her smile to hear Sunny and Will whisper, "I love you" in a quiet moment when they thought no one was listening. "I love you more," the other would reply before a quick nuzzle, out of their company's eye line. There was no greater joy for a mother than to have her child find true love, and in Will, Sunny had found just that.

Mabel watched them now as they rose from the car, shooing the kids around to the trunk where they began retrieving baskets and platters and jugs for the picnic. She admired Sunny with her raven hair and big, green eyes, looking very feminine in her cotton sundress splashed with daisies and pansies and a wide frock belt, as was the fashion.

Sunny wrinkled her eyes at the kids, smiling all the while as she issued orders like a drill sergeant. Meanwhile, Will shouldered the bulk of the burden with his strong arms and broad, smiling face.

Mabel often wondered if it was her son-in-law's profession that fueled his happy marriage. A veteran driver for Federal Truck Lines, based out of nearby Gainesville, Florida, Will was often gone for days at a time, crisscrossing the state and occasionally straying north into Georgia and South Carolina with his loads of supplies for the various retail industries that thrived throughout the land. They often said "absence makes the heart grow fonder." *Was that what kept their lifelong love alive?* Mabel thought as she rose at last to greet the arriving brood. Whatever the reason, her daughter was doing something right.

"Gramma," shouted the children, led by the teenager, Betty Jean, who gripped her in a bear hug just below her shoulders. Betty Jean was growing like a weed, her long coltish legs deeply tanned from a summer already more than halfway over and her pretty face the very picture of her mother's. Soon the lovely teen would be a head taller than her old grandmother, and it gave Mabel a bittersweet flutter in her heart to think that time had passed by so quickly. Why, it seemed only yesterday that the little tyke was in diapers and teething!

There was no time for such thoughts however, as the two boys took up where Betty Jean left off: Tony, the nine-year-old, gripped Mabel about her middle while little Jason, only three, took hold of her kneecap as if he hadn't seen her for years. Sadly, she knew just how he felt.

"Now let Gramma take a look at you all," she said as she wriggled from the loving embraces to gaze at her trio of grandkids. As always, Sunny had dressed the kids in summer finery. The boys in matching short and shirt sets and Betty Jean scrubbed fresh and looking wholesome in a sundress not quite as frilly, but nearly identical to her mother's. "I do declare you children are a sight for sore eyes. Why, Gramma barely recognized you it's been so long."

Sunny laughed at the not-so-subtle hint. "Only two weeks, Mama," she chided playfully as she reached in for a hug that let Mabel know her daughter had been missing her just as much.

"I know what you mean, Mabel," sighed Will heavily as he traded in a picnic basket for a hug from his favorite mother-in-law, "seems like it was a long time since I rested my eyes on the old homestead, but we're glad to be here now, right kids?"

The family clapped and Mabel smiled, leading them into the kitchen where pies were uncovered and iced tea doled out in long, tall glasses full of sugar and lemon. Thus refreshed, Mabel spied her antsy grandkids and knew what they were waiting for.

"All right," she sighed. "Now that you've made nice with Gramma, I'll tell you where you REAL favorites are: Uncle Fred and Uncle Ed are out in the backyard setting up a game of horseshoes. Your Aunt Dolores is supervising if you'd care to join Uncle Terry and Aunt Wanda."

Before the words were even from her mouth, Sunny's children scattered from the kitchen like buckshot, streaming through the tidy house. Mabel didn't breathe until she heard the screen door at the back of the house open and swing shut, with no breaking of glass along the way.

"Be careful what you wish for, Mama," Sunny joked as they retired to the porch to sip their iced tea, calling for Dolores to join them ast they waited for the rest of the families to arrive. "You always said you wanted a house full of grandchildren, well, now you've got them!"

Mabel laughed. "I guess your old Mama's getting set in her own ways, Sunny, But you're right; a broken dish is a small price to pay."

Will laughed halfway through his sweet, cold tea. "For Pete's sake, don't let *them* hear you say that, Mabel! You'll have nary a dish left by the end of the day."

The adults had a good time on the porch, idly catching up on each other's lives and then getting right down to business, that being the local gossip the others had missed in their months-long absence. Dolores came and joined the group on the porch. Will smiled good-naturedly before slipping away to supervise a loud game of horseshoes and letting Mabel and the girls chat. Soon the clank of old horseshoes could be heard from the backyard intermingled with the heady laughter of a family reunited.

Now Sunny sat a chair away, bright and smiling in her flowered sundress and telling her Mama all the joys and sorrows of a grown-up life. Mabel listened attentively, eager to offer a kind word or snippet of advice, as was a mother's wont. Dolores chatted about the baby-to-be. Together the women prattled away a half-hour that felt like two minutes, and soon, perhaps too soon, the rest of the brood drove up in a group of pick-up trucks and cars that contained Mabel's extended family.

Quickly a parade of daughters, sons-in-law, and grandchildren streamed toward Mabel's porch, where she stood all of 5'4", a titan of motherhood nonetheless who watched proudly as her loud, but loving children flocked to her with unbridled enthusiasm and open arms, clinging to her warmly as children of all ages, sizes, and shapes clasped her with respect and enthusiasm. She greeted each of them, offering sweet tea or lemonade on their way out back to join the rest of the children, who clamored eagerly for Uncle Ed's attention as he gave them piggy back rides and horseshoe lessons like the good uncle her son had become. Her daughter, Wanda, joined the women on the porch after sending her own kids to the backyard to join the rest of the gaggle.

All that afternoon the family spent time getting reacquainted, whether over glasses of cool refreshment or the glowing embers that had to be just right before the stubborn men would grill one frankfurter, let alone a hamburger or chicken. Those of Mabel's sons-in-law that were not supervising the cooking, took charge of making the homemade ice cream that would be the cap to their wonderful day together. Much discussion was made over the proper amount of rock salt and its ratio to crushed ice. Mabel heard it all with one ear as the laughter of grandchildren and the gossip of her daughters filled the other. She watched proudly as the men took turns cranking the churn in fifteen-minute shifts, though just like the women their mouths moved more than the lazily turned crank. The children, as eager as their fathers to be a part of the festivities, sat on a well-used oilcloth draped over the top of the churn, admiring their fathers' muscles as their arms labored over each turn of the crank, quickly wishing their turns were over as their little butts were getting very cold.

At last, the end of the churning coincided with the grilling of savory meats and vegetables and a late picnic lunch was served. While the men doled out equal portions of hamburgers and hot dogs, the women stood over a long picnic table covered with salads, buns, and condiments enough to feed a family twice as big. Children went along the table to fill their heaping plates and smiled at the mingling of watermelon juices and baked beans as they plopped their heavily-lade plates atop the family blankets Mabel had earlier weighted down.

After overseeing a platoon of plates and platters, bowls and spoons, Mabel at last grabbed her own plate and filled it sparingly, none too eager to take the last slice of anything, though she knew all too well her children would be eating leftovers the rest of the weekend and perhaps even lunch on Monday. Most families were staying over.

From the table to the porch to the blanket she walked, making sure everyone had enough mustard or napkins or lettuce or hot dogs. At last she sat on a rocker across from Ginny, her youngest daughter, who was on a swing with her handsome husband, Pete. Her two "lovebirds" had finished their lunch, carefully stacking their plates and covering them with napkins as they sat idly, canoodling and murmuring quietly about having a baby.

Mabel watched them enviously. To be so young and in love and just starting out in a new marriage, they reminded her so much of herself and Frank at that age, sitting on a similar porch swing and planning for the future. How differently her life had turned out from the way she had planned and yet so similar. If only Frank could see them now, she thought to herself for the hundredth time that day. And yet, she knew he was there; in spirit, in features, in name, in his legacy. And now here sat Ginny and Pete, enjoying a much-needed day off from the hardware store and sharing with Mabel their hopes for a child. More than anything, she knew, these two wanted a child. How it must have pained them to watch all the little ones, over a dozen, scampering from this blanket to that, pelting each other with watermelon seeds and already queuingined up for a shot at the first taste of ice cream. Though Ginny was proud of each of her three sisters and would never for a second begrudge them their loving families, Mabel knew her fondest desire was to start one of her own. For this, Mabel often prayed.

Finishing her plate and setting it to the side, she changed the subject. "Are y'all looking forward to your big fishing trip tomorrow?" Four of the group were going. She knew it had been the talk of her daughter's young group of friends for weeks now, and early tomorrow morning the trip would finally be here. A chartered boat, six couples sharing the cost of the charter, and a sunny Sunday in the weather forecast. Who wouldn't be looking forward to such a treat?

"Oh yes," said Ginny, though Mabel knew all-too-well it had been Pete's idea to go, "we're so excited we'll hardly sleep tonight."

"We better," Pete joked. "We're due at the dock before sunrise, so if we don't sleep tonight there'll be little chance of catching a few Z's in the morning."

"My, my," cooed Mabel, watching the sun as it rounded the sky toward the evening hour, "I hope you won't have to leave too terribly soon."

Pete and Ginny shared quick glances at each other. "Not too soon," Ginny reassured her mother.

"Just soon enough," Pete countered, eager to get a good night's sleep so as not to spoil the trip he'd been waiting for so long now.

Mabel sighed; it seemed like everyone just got here, now, with the picnic over, it was time to clean up. Ginny joined her as the women scouted the porch for empty plates and picked up napkins. This was soon done. Dishes were washed and dried. Then Mabel found herself a spot on the porch, leaving plenty of empty seats around her as, one by one, her daughters found their way to her side. As the men folk squared off against the oldest children in a friendly horseshoe competition, Mabel waited for her daughters to put their youngest ones down for a short, quiet nap. Meanwhile, she watched the young boys shooting marbles on one corner of the yard while, on the porch, the girls were playing with their favorite paper dolls.

As afternoon passed, Mabel's daughter Anne was the first to plop into a rocker beside her. "Here, Mama," she said, offering Mabel a glass of iced coffee. "I figure you could use a little fortification if you're to make it through the rest of the day."

Mabel took the glass graciously, enjoying the tempting southern after-dinner treat. "You always could read my mind, Anne," she said. "You sure you don't want one for yourself? Putting all those kids down must have you about ready for a nap, too."

At that precise moment Anne's husband, Bobby, appeared at the screen door with a second glass of iced coffee for his wife. "Madam," he offered with a horrible fake French accent, "your refreshment is served." Bobby grinned at Mabel before disappearing quickly back through the screen door to rejoin the marathon horseshoe game. Mabel noticed how Bobby had avoided slamming the door so as not to wake up the passel of sleeping children scattered throughout the living room and beyond, as too much food and excitement caught up with them.

Anne and Bobby, who had arrived from Madison the morning before for their usual three week visit, had no less than five kids and could use the break. Anne settled into the chair as mother and daughter quietly sipped their sweet drinks as the rest of the sisters filtered out onto the porch after their respective children had at last gone to nap.

"That should buy us a few hours of peace," sighed Wanda as she slumped into a rocking chair across from her mother. "Now, let the gabfest begin!"

And so it did. With the reassuring sounds of sleeping children in one ear and clanking horseshoes in the others, the Jennings women, no matter what their last names might currently be, they were always the Jennings women to Mabel, began a who's who of neighbors acquaintances, friends, and enemies. They talked for a couple of hours, until at last the first of the children roused from their pallets, rubbing sleepy eyes and straggling onto the porch to lean lazily against mother's laps and ask the eternal question, "What's next?"

"How about eating watermelon and climbing trees?" suggested Sunny. Yes, all of the kids were ready for that. After two hours the kids were back, what now?

Fortunately, Mabel was never one to be caught short where her grandchildren, or anyone else in her family for that matter, were concerned. Passing out a dozen jars with lids, Mabel turned off the porch lights and various sisters extinguished lamps throughout the sitting room until, at long last, darkness had come to Mabel's homestead. But not for long…

Invariably, the eerie glow of a twinkling firefly would emerge from the group of trees on Mabel's property. First one, then another, and then more and more, until at last the very night itself seemed alive with twinkling lights. Children ran about the yard, eagerly scooping live fireflies into their jars.

The older children, of course, led by Mabel's own teen, Ed, and Sunny's fourteen-year-old daughter, Betty Jean, collected dozens of fireflies, finally wandering off to the side of the drive with their glowing lanterns to talk about whatever teens talked about at that age. The little ones ran back and forth across the yard, eagerly bragging if they captured one or two and watching the curious insects raptly as they lay on the lawn, counting the seconds between each firefly's flash.

Thus the evening passes. The hunt continues, the parents talk, mosquitoes chase the kids inside and soon it is officially time for bed. Once again the process is repeated, as the youngest children crawl yawning into their assigned pallets, long since forgotten from naptime, and the older children adjourn to rooms throughout the house.

Mabel will watch all of the children until Sunday night, when her family of boaters will return from their fishing trip and collect their little ones for the short drive home. It is a chore she welcomed the moment she heard about it.

After a day of eating favorite food from each family, including fried chicken, baked beans, deviled eggs, corn on the cob and watermelon, everyone is full and satisfied. The adults talk and laugh a lot, remembering other family gatherings and especially "family jokes." One of the sisters recalled, "Remember the time Anne left her youngest one in the car for a few minutes because she was asleep, and when the kid woke up, she sat on the entire birthday cake Anne had left in the seat. That little on had pink icing all over her."

"Yeah, I remember," replied Anne. "Bobby even let the dog lick some of the icing off of her."

Then Mabel recalled, "Or that time Sunny and Ginny were over at our neighbor's house and the neighbors said, 'Oh, you and your old smart mama,' and Ginny told them, 'My Mama ain't smart.'"

"Oh yes she IS!" insisted all of the sons-in-law dutifully, causing the women to laugh all the harder.

The hour got later, with family tales and shared gossip, until at long last it is time for the early risers to part, with the morning's fishing trip in mind.

"We'll pick up the kids as soon as we get back, Mama," said Sunny, waving from the passenger seat as Will expertly exited the spot he so carefully chose hours earlier.

After that, some of the girls departed, one by one holding their husbands' hand on the way to their cars. Mabel watched them from the porch. She had enjoyed this perfect day, so much it was unbelievable. Taillights winked in the distance as her daughters return to their various homesteads, until at last Mabel was left, alone on the porch, with only the periodic flashing of fireflies to keep her company. She sighed, bending to the jars lined up carefully like luminaries up and down her front porch. One by one, jar after jar she released the fireflies back into the night. Just like her children, they are but a temporary joy to be savored and admired until they meet again.

CHAPTER 3

Dancing in the Dark

Fireflies were not the only things twinkling on this rarest of Saturday nights, as both Sunny and Will flirted mercilessly on the short drive home. It was a rare trip indeed, finding themselves making the return trip alone.

"Will you listen to that," whispered Sunny, her arm tenderly on Will's as the car crossed a deserted main street.

"Listen to what?" Will quipped. "Sounds like sweet, blissful silence to me!"

"My point exactly, Will. Isn't it heaven?"

"Heaven indeed, my dear," he responded. "Now come here my little angel, and plant one on your little cherub."

"Oh, Will," Sunny demurred, blushing in the dark and glad her husband of 16 years couldn't see it. "Not while you're driving. What would the papers make of it tomorrow if you have an accident?"

After a few more minutes, Will and Sunny settled into a comfortable silence, both anticipating their homecoming. "I do home the kids don't wear Mom out tomorrow." Sunny fretted as will rounded the corner on their street.

"Shoot," Will countered." "Mabel's probably spoiling them to beat the band as we speak. Why in the morning she will probably rouse those kids and make them take turns at the ice cream churn for round two!"

"You think?" Sunny asked.

Will noticed the tremor in her voice and, after parking the car in front of their darkened house, soothed her with a king word or two. "Darling," he whispered, looking into his wife's eyes, "there's not a thing for you to worry bout. It's Saturday night in Ocala and all is peaceful. Our kids are with the best babysitter in the world, and your Mom planning a Sunday the kids will be bragging on for years. Why, they may never want to come back!"

"Oh, Will," Sunny laughed, poking her husband in the ribs. They were surprisingly firm, and she was proud that Will, unlike many of her married friends' husbands, had retained his shape ever since playing tight end on the high school football team. Why, she bet he could still fit in his old uniform! "Don't say that," she continued, "as much as I enjoy the time alone with each other, honey, I look forward to seeing our babies again."

Will snorted. "They're far from babies, Sunny."

Sunny smiled. "They'll always be my babies to me, Will."

Will held his hands up in defeat. "All right then," he laughed. "Babies they will be. But for tonight, for one precious night, our babies are safe and sound in their grandmother's arms, and instead of sitting out here worrying about them, we should get our rear ends in that house and start celebrating."

Sunny rolled her eyes, but couldn't resist the opportunity to play hard to get; even if she didn't really mean it. "Oh, I don't know," she sighed, pretending to yawn as the two emerged from the car, footloose and fancy free. "All that eating, sitting, and eating really has me tuckered out."

Will's frown could be seen clear through the street light. "Nonsense, woman," he said playfully. "The night is young, and only just beginning."

"We'll see," she said noncommittally as the two started up the steps to the screened porch.

"Here then," he joked, pulling his beautiful wife into his arms and carrying her across the threshold.

Laughing their way through the doorway, both Will and Sunny stopped dead in their tracks and realized that, for the first time in weeks, possibly months, their house was serenely quiet. It is a magical moment for both husband and wife.

"Listen to that," Will cajoled. "More of that magical, marvelous silence."

"I know how to fix that," said Sunny, walking straight to the radio and switching it on to their favorite station. Along the way she turned out the lights, and went so far as to light the dinner candles.

"Sweetie," Will sighed, nodding toward the flickering glow of the romantic candlelight, "this must be a special night indeed."

From the radio, the effortless strains of Frank Sinatra oozed with his rendition of "Mam'selle." As Will stopped at the front door, locking it, then placing his car keys, as always, on the sideboard in the foyer, Sunny hummed along with the bittersweet lyrics of one of the year's most popular songs.

"Ah, I love it when we hear this song, darlin'," Will said as the song ended and another one began.

"Let's dance, Will," Sunny chirped.

Smiling, Will joined her. As the song progressed, the dance of two became more intimate. They sensed the eagerness in their bones, the lightness on their feet. The slight trembling in each others arms as the song at last ended. Sunny said, "Let's go to bed and *not* get some sleep."

Will laughed and said, "You've got a deal, honey, blow out the candles."

Hugging, they walked into the bedroom slowly. It was a short trip, but the couple enjoyed every second of it. Sunny reached to close the bedroom door, a holdover, perhaps, from raising three kids and only occasionally getting a rare moment of privacy. But Will stopped the door from closing entirely, whispering, "I love how the moonlight looks on your face."

Sunny melted in his arms, nuzzling his neck and smelling the bittersweet mixture of his everyday male smell with the sweet, sentimental smells of the day: watermelon seeds, fried chicken, the hugs of their children. It was truly an intoxicating scent...a male smell.

With the curtains half drawn, the radio nearly—just nearly—drowning out the sound of their loving heartbeats, and the moonlight flickering across their smiling faces, the husband and wife undressed each other without reserve or shyness. As the evening stepped into liquid, they took their time, lingering over buttons and buckles and zippers and sashes. They had always been playful, gentle lovers, and being alone in the house for the first time in months, though it felt like years, they lingered over every detail of each other's bodies.

They nuzzled, caressed, and soothed each other as the evening fell outside their windows. Inside it swirled without end, as clothes lay in heaps on the floor as Sunny moaned, as pleased with the sound of her own voice as she was with the man who was making her use it. Naked and alone, the two fell into bed; within minutes the sheets were entangled like a noose at one end, with the writing couple ecstatic and sweat dampened, their young bodies glistening in the moonlight as they continued to caress and love each other through the evening.

By now their bodies were as pleasant and familiar as their daily routines, and yet on this strange, unexpected, magical night, the two gasped with excitement at the newness of each other. New sounds, new features, new tricks, new angles to explore and caress as the minutes, then hours, slipped away. Even afterward, lying spent and crumpled in each other's arms, husband and wife could not part. They lay nestled, like spoons in a drawer, as Sunny sighed into

Will's ear and he smiled at the tickling, ecstatic sensation her breath caused in his ear. Wordlessly, they lay in each other's arms, fresh from their lovemaking, reveling in the odd quiet of the midnight hour, anticipating their Sunday outing with family and friends.

At last, Will sighed, giving up the last of their dreamtime. "You know there'll be heck to pay tomorrow morning, Sunny," he said, moments from sleep.

"Honey," she murmured, "it was worth every minute."

"That it was, my dear," he said, though she had already lapsed into the deep sleep of contented lovers everywhere. "That it was."

Then, too, Will drifted off into a peaceful rest, dreaming of waves and hooks and cold drinks and warm sunshine and a day spent on the water with his one and only love, Sunny, by his side.

Morning would come too quickly…

CHAPTER 4

Breathing Lessons

Across town, the two "lovebirds" had returned home from the picnic and wasted little time enjoying "dessert." As they stood at the doorway, Ginny could wait no longer to cross the threshold of their humble abode.

"Pete," she urged in a tense whisper, as if their sleeping neighbors might hear. "Whatever is taking so long?" He heard the hoarse whisper of desire in her throat, a sound that often crept up at the most inopportune moments.

"I'm sorry, Petey," he crooned, suddenly all thumbs. Ginny blushed in the dark at Pete's special nickname for her; it was such a term of endearment, a special code between the two lovers, used mainly during such intimate moments as this one.

As he turned to answer her, the key finally slid in the lock and the door swung open, the porch light illuminating the living room and alerting the two lovebirds to the presence of their masters.

"Oh, Pete," Ginny sighed.

"Oh, Petey," he sighed back, ignoring the keys still hanging from the door and wrapping his love up in the strength of his broad arms. She felt so tiny there, warm against his solid chest as they moved inside.

Her breath came soft and hot across his neck even as her fingers trembled through the act of unbuttoning his cotton summer shirt. He responded in kind, slipping off her blouse and watching as the night air bathed her smooth, pale skin in a ripple of goose pimples illuminated by a slice of moonlight peeking through the clouds. As the two disrobed, their pet lovebirds began chirping at the embracing couple, unused to such wanton displays of affection.

Ginny laughed, and between kisses lavished on her husband's cleft chin, giggle, "We have an audience, Pete."

"Not for long, Petey," said her husband, picking his shirt off the floor and tossing it expertly over the birdcage.

The two dissolved into laughter even as their clothes pooled about them on the floor. Together they collapsed onto the bed, the darkness of their bedroom as husband and wife explored long familiar nooks and crannies of each other's bodies, the leisure and laughter of the day culminating in a closeness only man and wife can truly share.

After their love had been spent they lay in each other's arms, silently counting their blessings even as they wandered in and out of sleep. Pleasant dreams were soon cut short when Pete noticed the telltale wheezing of one of Ginny's asthma attacks. She sat beside him, too weakened by her shortness of breath to reach the steam kettle in the kitchen the doctor had prescribed for her. He ran to get it, pulled her desperately to the table, and minutes later filled a bowl with steaming water from the kettle and covered her head with a towel.

When the steam had finally taken effect and Ginny was able to speak, she thanked her husband. Only then did he take a breath of his own. "Petey," he said calmly, spying the clock on the bedside nightstand and noticing it was well past three in the morning, "are you okay?"

She nodded, still not ready to speak. He waited patiently by her side, trembling with fear that his young wife should be saddled by such a condition. Only hours earlier she had been a vibrant, sensuous woman, undressing him in the doorway of their home, for crying out loud! Now she was barely recognizable, pale and shaken and drenched in sweat from her middle of the night battle with lungs that betrayed her whenever, wherever they felt like it.

He waited for her breathing to return to normal, and eventually it did. Only then did he offer, "You know, maybe we should cancel our fishing trip. We have to get up in a few hours and—"

"I'll hear none of that," she said with a renewed strength to her voice. "You've been looking forward to that trip for weeks now and I'm not going to let a little thing like asthma get in the way of our fun day together."

"But honey," he argued, "what if something happens? What if, God forbid, you have an attack and we're in the middle of the ocean? What then?"

"Then," she said," in my bedroom or on a boat, I'm not going to let this condition dictate my life. We're young, Pete, we should live like it."

Pete merely shook his head, and said no more. His wife might have been a mere slip of a girl, physically speaking, but she could also be stubborn and willful. When she set her mind to something, whether it be opening up a business together or going on this fishing trip, there was no stopping her. It was what he loved, and feared, the most about her...

Trying to break the grim pall of concern that had washed over her husband's face of late, Ginny joked, "I always said you took my breath away, Pete. Now you know I meant it!"

He frowned, "That's not funny, Ginny."

They sat there like that, slivers of moonlight slipping through the blinds as the night ticked inexorably on. "We've got to get up in a few hours, Ginny. Do you think you can get back to sleep?"

"Only if you hold me tight, Pete," she sighed, slipping into his arms as he slid the covers back over her pale, trembling body. "Only if you hold me..."

He did, and after several minutes of tossing and turning, she at last succumbed to the exhaustion that often followed one of her late night attacks. He fretted over the trip; his concerns were real and her stubbornness was maddening. Half of him wanted to throw off the covers and turn off the alarm, but the other half knew she had climbed into his arms to avoid him doing just that. He smiled at her strength of will and her cunning wiles. He would hope for the best. It was only supposed to be a half-day on the water. She was right, as always.

"What could go wrong?" he thought as sleep, at long last, claimed him as well...

CHAPTER 5

Sam and Analee Meet Abbot and Costello

Analee and Sam strolled arm in arm from the movie theater, silently milling with the crowds as another lazy Saturday night passed quietly in their small Florida town. Nodding to strangers, smiling to friends, they stood next to the darkened ticket booth comparing notes on their favorite scenes. The crowd was unusually thick that night, perhaps owing to the popularity of the early summer hit they'd all just seen, *Abbot & Costello Meet Frankenstein.* The mix of horror and humor proved a heady combination for the buzzing crowd, who were still laughing over the film's funniest moments as they scattered on the quiet city street.

Behind them the Marion Theater closed up shop for the night, the heavy glass double doors locking with a thud after the last audience member streamed from the lobby and the concessionaires bagging up sleeves of pop-corn for tomorrow's matinees, where kids who had saved their pennies all week would stream through the doors, so eager to see the week's latest double feature. They wouldn't mind if the popcorn was just a tad stale.

Meanwhile, the late show was over and the ushers were eager to get home, but for Analee and Sam the second half of their night was just beginning. With his studies over the for week, the stresses and occasional boredom of her job far behind her, Analee and Sam looked forward to the next morning's fishing trip, but were young enough to turn the weekend trip into a holiday of sorts. Their celebration had already started.

The June breeze was softly warm, almost cool as the couple followed the last of the hungry stragglers down three darkened storefronts to stop at Aunt Jayne's Café for a bite to eat. At this time of the night the normally lively little eatery was mostly empty, but as late-night diners fresh from the Marion filtered through the door in twos, threes, and fours, the wait staff and cooks perked up for the night's last big rush.

The two took their favorite booth by the window, sitting across from each other and holding hands as the after-movie crowd settled and the waitress's, complete in aprons and nametags, divvied up the tables. Popular music of the era was pumped into the dining area from a behemoth jukebox stationed just between the men's and women's restrooms and during slow times the waitresses on shift often cut a rug to the big band tunes of Benny Goodman and Tommy Dorsey just to pass the time or make the tasks of their work pass all the more quickly.

For now, though, pencils were retrieved from behind ears and order pads pulled from apron pockets as the night shift moved from table to table, scribbling down orders for root beer floats and French fries, the orders plenty big enough to share. Sam and Analee had no reason to look at the menu. After ordering, Sam exclaimed to Analee, "Cheeseburgers and cherry cokes are better here than any place in town."

She agreed, but then quickly excused herself to "powder her nose." Sam suspected he knew the real reason she'd leapt up from the table so soon after sitting down, and his suspicions were confirmed as she stopped at a table of friends from work on the way to the ladies room.

"Finally," she whispered to her comrades in arms as they struggled to draw one of Aunt Jane's notoriously thick strawberry shakes through three straws. When her girlfriends looked nonplussed, perhaps wondering if she'd gotten a new haircut or skirt, Analee pushed out her chest, all the better for them to admire the fraternity pin Sam had bestowed upon her just before the movie.

"You got pinned!" one of her friends exclaimed as the other two joined in to share their congratulations. They all waved to Sam, who sat blushing on his side of the booth, not quite used to—and none too fond of—being the center of attention. Still, as Analee bent to chat with her friends, he couldn't help but be proud of his decision. She'd been wanting something more serious, a commitment of sorts and they both agreed "getting pinned" was the next step. Neither was ready to get married, and the symbolic gesture of her wearing a simple pin for each other's loyalty and devotion seemed the next best thing.

Now the two could relax and enjoy the bliss of young couple-dom, and yet still manage to avoid the serious finality of saying, "I do."

Sam liked Analee, perhaps even loved her, but they both felt too young to take that next big step. Now they were both happy, and it showed on Analee's face. He watched as she talked, her eyes alight with pride and excitement. She couldn't seem to stop smiling; bright, white teeth flashing every time she smiled or opened her mouth to speak. He admired the long legs poking out of her calf-length skirt. The legs strong from her weekly games of tennis or daily bike ride to and from work, her skin bronzed and supple from the Florida sun. His Analee, nicknamed Leesie.

Her blond hair cascaded across her young, slim shoulders, swaying this way and that as she shook her head modestly in response to a friend's question or nodded it effusively toward another. She looked back frequently to check on Sam, aware their night together would soon end and none too eager to waste it chatting with her friends. Soon enough she retuned to their table and he ribbed her about "forgetting to powder her nose."

"You silly," she giggled, sipping the cherry coke that had been set in front of her place in her absence. "I couldn't get pinned and NOT show it off, now could I? You know how the girls at work have been teasing me about 'settling down.' I just had to tell them this was about as settled as I, as we, were ready to get."

When Sam didn't respond right away, Analee pressed him. "Was I wrong, honey?"

He smiled. "Not a bit. I think it's great we can discuss things like equals and not hide things or pretend with each other. It's important to go into our relationship with our eyes wide open, our minds too."

As their waitress slid two heaping platters filled to the brim with sizzling cheeseburgers and piping hot French fries, Analee quipped, "Let's not forget our mouths wide open, too!"

Analee, still full from a little too much popcorn during the movie—she always ate when she was scared—only managed to finish half of her burger and but a few of her fries before sliding her plate across to Sam. He nodded approvingly, mouth too full to thank her verbally, and she marveled at his appetite. But then, he was still a growing boy. And was he ever! Tall, dark and handsome certainly described her man to a "T," and never was she happier than when showing off her man about town.

All the girls at work were jealous, her high school pals, too, and wearing Sam's pin was the crowning achievement on their eight months worth of courtship. She'd wear it proudly, and reflected on what it meant for their future. Sam was still in college after serving in the Navy. She was proud that he'd served his country, as many young men from town had, but even prouder that he'd put his brain to match his brawn and was now making use of the government's offer to send him to college in return for serving dutifully. Between his school and her job for the Marion County Agriculture Department, the two were busier than ever, and she knew the pin was only a gesture in some of her friends' eyes, but to her it signified a starting point in their shared future. His pin was her badge of honor, and she'd wear it proudly.

After dinner they strolled home leisurely, enjoying the night air and the chance to walk off their heavy meal. Sam held her hand, it felt so small in his, and matched her step for step as they left the stiff concrete of town and lingered over the shortcut to her mother's house. They chatted of little things, and big ones: the movie, their life, their friends, the superiority of cherry coke to lemonade, his classes, her job, their future. They were young, and in love, but in no hurry.

She was smart enough to be honest with Sam, and he respected her enough to be just as honest back. She was a modern woman: educated, smart, young, and employed. He was a modern man, a veteran, seeking his degree and a better life, either just for himself or for both of them. Much like their strides just fit, their personalities meshed as well. She appreciated his sense of humor, he valued her mind, and together the two matched their outer beauty with an inner confidence that demanded respect and loyalty of one another. For now, it was enough.

As the two lingered on Analee's front porch, they flirted mercilessly and kissed tenderly, before Sam, ever the gentleman turned and started the trek to his parents' house across town. It was late, and though temptation suggested they linger, both knew they'd be seeing each other in but a few short hours, making their parting that much easier to take.

Before drifting off to sleep that night, Analee rested Sam's pin on her nightstand. In the pale moonlight filtering between the slats of her closed blinds, its shiny radiance soothed her into a dreamless slumber.

As her alarm rang early, far too early for her liking anyway, the next morning, the pin was the first thing she saw. As expected, it caused her heart to leap, quickly followed by her body as it turned off the clanging clock next to her bed, in order not to wake her mother down the hall. She dressed quickly, illuminated only by the small bulb in her closet so her mother would not be tempted to rise so very early. Analee smiled at the colorful, one piece bathing suits lining her shelves.

To supplant her income, and as a change of pace from her routine desk job, Analee worked most weekends during the summer as a model at the nearby Silver Springs theme parks. The bathing suits were her costume, her only costume, as she emerged at appointed times to pose for pictures with the well-meaning and appreciative tourists. Standing beside a palm tree or a pretty flowing plant, Analee's comely legs, sun-drenched face, and brilliant smile were the prefect souvenir for the many visitors now streaming to Central Florida during the post-war tourist boom. Sometimes she swam under a glass bottom boat.

She'd had the job since high school, and had long since forgotten the number of pictures she'd adorned, but certainly by now they were in the thousands. Like Sam's pin, the job was another validation of her self-worth. She'd long since learned, thanks mostly to her mother's good advice and patient ear, that it wasn't enough to just be pretty, but in the modern world women would need to be smart as well. Even at her tender age, Analee felt certain she was both.

And still, her modesty remained in tact. She knew too well that looks were fleeting, and thus had wanted to make sure that Sam loved her for more than just her long blond hair or even longer legs. Her figure, like all women's, would fade. Would Sam's love fade just as quickly once that happened? She wasn't sure, but such were the doubts that made her none too eager to rush into a marriage before Sam had finished college and established himself in his career. That was only a few years away. Certainly, by then, she would know her heart and, she hoped, Sam would know his. That left them plenty of time to settle into their relationship.

At the moment, she was just glad she was dressing for a relaxing day cruise and not her weekend job at Silver Springs. With the day off stretching long and carefree in front of her, she finished dressing and made her way slowly, through the dark, into the kitchen. There, propped in the fridge, was a sack lunch her mother had made for her and Sam the night before. Peeking inside, she spotted her favorite: cheese sandwiches, raw vegetables, and fresh fruit. None too eager to wake her mother, but knowing she'd regret it if she didn't even peek in on her, Analee tiptoed down the darkened hall to her bedroom.

Cracking open the door, Analee was not too surprised to see her mother, the lightest of sleepers, half-propped in bed, her nightgown alternating shades of pink and white. "Have a good time, Leesie," her mother told her, whispering so as not to rouse herself too much. It was far too early to rise, but she'd wanted to wish her daughter off as much as Analee had wanted her to.

Analee crept into the room, hugging her as she replied, "I'll be home before you know it. Bye, now."

As she watched her mother sink back, she heard the sound of Sam's car pulling up in the driveway and hurried from the silent house to meet him. He was up and out to greet her, taking her sack lunch and tucking it in the back as he held the door open for her.

"Leesie," he wolf whistled, taking in the cut of her latest fashions and marveling at this heavenly beauty who'd agreed to wear his pin, "You look great!"

Analee blushed beneath her deep summer tan, standing tall in her white summer shorts and red and white shirt in the latest style. Her collar hugged her slim, tan throat and her seasonally short sleeves allowed her to appear both comfortable and casual at the same time. She and Sam were dressed in the same colors, his thickly muscled legs and flat stomach filling out his crisp white slacks and his firm arms and chest straining against his red sports shirt.

"I think we match perfectly, don't you?" she asked as she settled in beside him.

"I sure do," replied Sam as he got back in the car, "but don't forget the piece de resistance!" With that, her beau donned a jaunty sailor's cap, completing his nautical theme and framing his handsome face with its white brim.

With a smile on his face and one arm around her, they headed to the boat dock, the headlights of his secondhand jalopy slicing through the early morning darkness as they wound their way on to the Yankee Town Dock, some 45 minutes away. As they drove, both young people agreed: It was going to be a lovely day.

Leaving the bedroom, on the way to their kitchen, Lois and Bill met up with Lois' Mom, Carol. Both said, "good morning." Carol replied, "Morning, I hope you don't mind my being up to see you off."

"Oh, no," replied Lois, "You know how nervous I am about being out on the water."

Carol understandingly said, "I know you remember how your best friend, Little Dottie, drowned when y'all were just nine, but, honey, there will be no roots for you to get your hair caught on like there was at that old swimming hole."

"I know, Momma, I know. It just stays with me, us not finding her in that pond for so long a time. If we had just known her hair was caught on those old roots."

"Sweetheart," Bill quietly said, "If we are going we had better leave soon." Seeming to shake herself out of the old memories, Lois responded, "Yes you are right, we do need to go. Bye, Momma, We'll be back late afternoon."

"By now, dear," Carol replied.

In a home a few miles away, Lex and Lacey were getting ready.

"Oh Lex," asked Lacey, "Do you think I'll get sunburned? I will just hate it if I am burned and peel! I will just be so upset."

Now Lex, being a smart man and not wanting to make waves, replied, "Honey, you took your hat and sunglasses to Silver Springs, you took good care of the kids, they didn't get burned and your parents didn't get burned. I want you to be happy you are going with me." Lex, being that smart man, knew if his wife wasn't happy, he wouldn't be happy.

"I know! I know!" said Lacey. "I just want to look my best. I have a new out-fit and new shoes and we have a new car. I am happy!" she said emphatically. "Well, are you ready? Let's go, we can't be the last ones there."

"Don't move," said Kate, "maybe if I get up really slow, maybe I won't get sick.

"Okay, sweetie," said Hank, "anything to help out." But even as she slipped ever so slowly out of bed, it hit her. Running now, she just made it to the bathroom.

"Need any help, Babe?"

Kate only held up a hand over her head. This they had done before, actually for many weeks now.

"I'll go make tea and toast for you, okay?"

Raising her hand over her head again was Kate's only answer. In a little while the tea was done and so was Kate, at least for this morning. Later, packing to go, Hank asked one more time, "Are you sure you want to go?"

"Oh yes, I'm fine now. Anyway, I have an appointment early in the morning with Dr. Meade."

CHAPTER 6

Sittin' on the Dock of the Bay

Sunday morning dawned clear and bright for a dozen of Ocala's longtime residents, though it was well before dawn and not nearly as light as most of them would normally prefer. Still, this was a special day for them all and each amateur angler rose eagerly from bed. Houses suddenly childless reverberated with the pleasant strains of silence as parents played hooky, at least for a day, from rousting little ones and standing sentinel as they brushed their teeth or made their beds. Showers sprang to life and toes were stubbed as early risers battled unfamiliar corners in the dark. Outfits were chosen, more quickly for the men, who were more interested in comfort than style, knowing a long, hot day faced them; more slowly for the women, who looked forward to such outings to show off the latest summer fashions, if only to each other on this male-dominated day.

While the men folk busied themselves with tackle and rods and hauling down fishing hats from closet shelves, the women busied themselves with strong coffee as they bent over kitchen counters, assembling packed lunches to be consumed aboard the boat. Up and down Ocala's tree-lined streets lights came on. At the house just down the street from Sunny and Will, Pete and Ginny were preparing for their long, fun Sunday out to sea.

Pete would lean in and out of his closet, jauntily applying this cap or that for Ginny's approval as she tried to fix a box lunch for their trip. Ever serious about the tiniest of details, down to the crust cut off of her sandwiches and carefully sliced watermelon, a picnic favorite this time of year, Ginny was never too busy to offer advice to her fashion-challenged husband.

"Too stiff," she'd say, "Too broad."

"Oh, that was a gift, Pete. You don't want to mess that up with fish guts!"

A few doors down, a crisis of another sort was brewing as her sister and Will, rising later than the rest, for obvious reasons, struggled to play catch-up in the packing of lunch and dressing departments. Sunny, wearing a sundress and sandals, was finally wrapping up her lunch for the trip, which consisted of thick, homemade ham and mustard sandwiches. Pickles and boiled eggs finished out the menu. She had been tempted to add Will's favorite, her much-reputed potato salad, but was afraid of what the hot Florida sun might do to Will's favorite ingredient: mayonnaise. Though it was a staple of their daily cooking, most Florida women knew almost instinctively at birth that the sun and mayonnaise didn't mix, and much like wearing white after fall, they avoided using the popular southern staple unless an icebox was near.

Meanwhile, Will was dawdling in the bathroom, as always, fixing the part in his hair and flossing his broad, white teeth. "The vanity of men," Sunny sighed as she put the finishing touches on her boxed lunch and finished the last of her breakfast, which consisted of a toasted peanut butter and jelly sandwich. They were due to leave any minute, and she knew Pete and Ginny were scheduled to swing by and pick them up on the way. Sighing, Sunny called out to Will, "Please hurry in the bathroom, honey, or you'll be too late to eat anything before Pete and Ginny pick us up."

Like most men, Will only thought of food when it was too late and he was already hungry. At last Will emerged from the bathroom, resplendent in his fishing gear and lucky ball cap, but just as Sunny offered up his long-ignored sandwich there came from the driveway a familiar toot on the horn. They quickly gathered their things and dashed out to meet their family; breakfast forgotten, but not for long.

Just as Will prepared to hop into the back of Pete's car, his brother-in-law, buddy, and neighbor quipped, "Aren't you forgetting something, pal?"

Will sighed, "If you're here to remind me that I missed 'the most important meal of the days,' Sunny here's already beat you to it."

"Not that, partner," said Pete. "I meant your sign. Take a gander," with a steady hand, Pete pointed down a couple houses to where a cardboard sign was propped, just so, on his screen door.

"Too right," grinned Will as he unfolded himself from the car to retrieve his own cardboard, hand-lettered sign saying "Gone Fishing." He promptly hung it on his screen door so anyone stopping by could see the sign, and know where he and Sunny would be for the rest of the day.

"Thanks pal," he said admiring his handiwork as he got back into the car.

"What are friends for, right?" smiled Pete as he gunned the engine and drove off into the dark of night. As they passed their friends' and family members' houses along the way, similarly homemade signs were propped on several screen doors. Although it wasn't possible, of course, it appeared most of Ocala had "Gone Fishing!"

Still, in the early morning darkness, the foursome were the first passengers to arrive at the rustic boat dock in Yankeetown. As they bumped along the old rutted roads, the men held onto their hats while the women kept watch over the picnics in their laps. The old Florida scene was made even more bucolic by the waning moonlight. The creeping light helped to illuminate the sandy parking lot as Pete angled his car in the first spot leaving plenty of room for those fishermen and women still to come.

The buzzing of mosquitoes and the belching of frogs hidden deep in the underbrush were the first sounds to greet the two couples as Pete shut off the engine and rolled up the windows.

As sisters and husbands emerged from the car, stretching their limbs against the steamy morning air, they admired the weeping willows and hanging moss that seemed to be everywhere in all the trees.

Dense scrub brush and thick, waist high palmettos dotted the landscape as the foursome stared up at the leaning bait shack that squatted squarely in the middle of the Yankeetown dock.

It was a rambling affair, featuring odd corners and thick windows on both walls of the tin roofed building that, at first glance, threatened to slide off into the murky brown water lapping mere yards from the broad, open front door.

Hand-painted signs featured night crawlers and shrimp for pennies a dozen, but as the cost of their day package included both bait and tackle, the men ignored the signs and instead eyed the haphazard architecture.

"I hope the boat's in better shape," whispered Will to Pete as they at last stepped foot on the dock.

"Me too," Will replied, smiling to himself. Both men knew the rustic nature of a Florida fishing trip was part and parcel of its charm, but it didn't stop them from a little friendly joshing nonetheless.

It was, but not much. The "Hazy Days" was white with red trim, 38-feet long and twelve-years-old. There was a cabin in the middle of the deck and a ship's wheel was up front in a small enclosure. The small cabin contained a toilet, two bunks, and the engine in the floor.

It sat high in the water, moored by sun bleached and worn lines affixed to the equally weathered dock. Like many boats of its age, the "Hazy Days" was a time-tested if not eye-friendly craft.

A paint job was in order, but otherwise the boat seemed sound and sturdy. Compared to the smaller craft dotting the Yankeetown harbor, it seemed the jewel of the fleet and eyeing it made the men fell secure.

They only hoped their wives agreed…

Already on board the boat were Capt. L. B. Wilson and his fishing guide, Buck Gibbs. Both men greeted the foursome warmly, eager to get an early start on the day and thankful for the two couple's promptness.

"Fine day for it," said Captain Wilson, helping the women aboard with hands as big and broad as they were tough and leathery. A lifetime in the sun had weathered the hearty 34-year-old into a bronzed and able seaman, and he loved his job.

Though the Hazy Days had only been his for six months, owning a boat had long been a dream and it was now a testament to his perseverance and drive that he'd managed to fulfill his lifelong dream before his 35th birthday.

Buck Gibbs, his trusted friend and able fishing guide, was happy to serve alongside his friend and captain. Buck was a weathered soul who'd been on the open water more than he'd been on dry land.

His gray-blue eyes and deep-set crow's feet were sanded in place by years of salty spray. His sun-bleached blond hair had become a perch for a seaman's cap and made him the very picture of an "old salt," though he was a bit younger than his captain he was every bit as experienced.

As Buck helped the ladies stow their picnics in the ice bin beneath bench seats, Wilson chatted amicably with the men about their day at sea.

"Any of you fellows ever fought a grouper before?" the captain asked Pete and Will.

Both men nodded as Pete bragged, "We try to go out at least a couple times a year. I guess you could kind of call it a tradition."

The captain nodded, seeing repeat customers in his future if the day went as planned. "Well I hope y'all consider the Hazy Days for your next outing, too."

Bill and Lois Saunders were the next passengers to arrive. Always being on time was important to a barber, even on his day off! As they approached the dock, Bill could sense that Lois's already unsteady nerve was beginning to waver.

Lois loved to fish, but she had never been on a big boat, or, for that matter, a large body of water before. She was more familiar with the local docks and waterways dotting Ocala, and was fine when seated on dry land with a line in the water and a cool glass of lemonade at her side.

The open water, especially when she could no longer see the shoreline, made her nervous and she'd shared her fears with Bill on more than one occasion. She was skittish and reluctant to go, and unhappy about the prospect of leaving dry land.

Halfway to the dock she paused, sorely tempted to call the trip off and drive back home. Bill sensed her hesitation, and turned toward her in the sandy parking lot of the now bustling harbor.

"Still fighting those butterflies I see," Bill teased her. "Honey, don't worry. You know I'll take good care of you. Why, I'd never let anything bad happen to you. Ever."

"He watched as several emotions crossed her face at once. A barber always knows his audience, senses when to joke and josh or when to listen, senses just how short he wants his hair or close his shave, and in this case Bill knew Lois needed a little something to take her mind off that big, hulking boat and that crooked, yawning dock.

"Honey, you remember how we met. You were still a senior in high school and I was just learning how to be a barber. You used to pass the shop twice a day, and I'd make sure to look up both times, no matter who was in my chair or how much I needed to learn.

"It was love at first sight, Lois, I swear by it. When I finally had the nerve to be waiting outside one day on your way home from school, leaning against that barber pole, I could tell you were interested in me, too. Now we're married, and our kids are at home with you mom. Why we haven't been apart for one single night since we wed, and I don't plan on parting ways now.

"If I wasn't 100% certain this trip was a good idea, why darling, I never would have suggested it to you. Fact is, I know how much you love to fish and I think this could open up a whole new world for us."

He watched a tentative smile cross her face, put there by the memory of their young, intense, undying glove. "You know the store's been doing well this year, honey. Why, I thought we might even invest in a little boat, you know. Keep it docked here at Yankeetown and take the kids out fishing when they're old enough. A real family affair.

"So let's not think of this as all doom and gloom, honey. Let's think of it as a test run for our own fishing excursions. Look, Pete and Ginny and Will and Sunny are already here, let's not rain on their parade, huh?"

"Why, they wouldn't have agreed to come if they didn't think the boat was safe and the weather was right. In no time they'll have you talking like there's no tomorrow and laughing to beat the band. What do you say, honey?"

She nodded hesitantly, but her feet were already moving forward, stepping firmly onto the dock and no longer wavering as she greeted the captain with a warm smile as he helped hoist her aboard.

Bill followed, greeting the captain, his mate, and his friends with his usual energy and aplomb before turning his attention back to Lois.

He took her by the hand, sensing it shake despite her forced bravado, and felt a little twinge of guilt tug at his heart. *Maybe this wasn't such a great idea after all*, he thought as he led her straight to a bench near the back of the boat, where they sat down together.

Looking down with a smile, Bill asked, "Honey, are you okay? After a slight hesitation, she nodded affirmatively, and he rubbed her hand as if to say, "Good girl."

He knew she needed time to adjust to her new surroundings. Lois was shy, but that was what he so loved about her. For every outgoing cell in his body hers were just as quiet and gentle.

Like many loving couples, they tempered each other. She calmed him down and he picked her up, boosting her when she was down as often as she soothed him when he was edgy or tense, working up about some unsatisfied customer at the shop or some grim piece of world news he'd heard between big band songs on the radio behind his chair.

He tucked her on the brim of her fashionable hat, admiring her slim body beneath her summer shorts and cool, cotton blouse and her long brown hair brushing her shoulders.

She smiled up at him from under her jaunty brim and then he took the fried chicken and boiled eggs and placed them in the ice bin under the seat cushions. She watched him, joking with Will and was resigned to the day and as eager to spend it with her good friends and family as she was, frankly, to have it over with.

Still, looking at Bill joking with his buddies and following the captain around to get a five cent tour of the vessel, she knows to leave now would crush his plans and ruin a day he's looked forward to for so long now. She thinks of their three children, wondering what they are doing at that very moment.

How she longed to be with them, safe on dry ground. Even now the gentle lapping of the waves beneath the still-docked boat sent ripples through her already nervous stomach.

Looking up to steady herself and take on last look at "dry land," she smiles to see Hank and Kate Mays ambling up to the boat, their squeaky new deck shoes clean and bright against the weathered planks of the dock's old wood.

As the captain and his mate helped the newly arrived couple aboard Lois got up and sat with them. Bill smiled, eager to see Lois relax and enjoy her day. He yawned, realizing his anxiousness for this day to arrive has cost him precious sleep.

Lex and Lacey Ross arrive next, and are happy to see old friends. They join them on the deck, milling about pleasantly and getting the lay of the land as the inevitably good-natured ribbing about "sleepyhead" and "the early bird catches the grouper" make them feel right at home.

Together the assembled couples mill about, filling the broad, open deck at the back of the boat and splitting up into twos or threes, much like they might at a backyard barbecue or Sunday cookout.

The captain and first mate smile to see their customers. They know this brief but important interlude in shallow water and without waves is vital for the "Landlubbers" to not only get acquainted with the boat but likewise to get their sea legs before striking out into open water.

Though the winds are slight and bearing from the southeast, the captain knows any open water is an adjustment for "civilians," as he calls them, and he's none too eager for any of them to get seasick on him—or his new boat!

Finally, the ship is ready and so are it's passengers. The men cluster about, eyeing the rising sun and eager to get to it. The women sit and chit-chat, comparing lunches and outfits and rolling their eyes at the men, who are now chomping at the bit to get their hands around a rod and reel and fight the legion of grouper who thrive 25 to 35 miles off the Florida coast.

At long last, Analee and Sam make their appearance, looking young and dapper in their nautical attire and beaming at the thought of their day aboard the big boat with family and friends. As they take a seat near the back of the boat, they stop to put sandwiches, wrapped in waxed paper, in the ice bin.

Sam eagerly joins the men, apologizing for their tardiness immediately to avoid their good-natured taunts and barbs, but it is already too late. Bill, the resident comedian, starts in immediately and Sam takes the ribbing as his due.

From their post, the women immediately spot Analee's shiny new pin, affixed to the wide lapel of her breezy, red blouse and congratulate her—and Sam, who blushes to match his red shirt.

Their arrival completes the passenger group of twelve…

The excitement of the trip is shared by all the passengers as they board the fishing boat. Talk of fishing fills the air as lunches and drinks are secured for the trip out to open water. As final preparations are underway, the captain and his mate busy themselves securing the tackle and bait they'll need for the day at sea.

They work in comfortable tandem, sending unspoken signals and working easily with each other. It is said the relationship between a captain and his mate is similar to that of an old married couple, and despite the incongruity of these salty, weathered men being compared to man and wife, the easy way they share the brunt of the duties and communicate without talking proves the cliché an apt one.

Watching the last minute burst of activity on the weathered surface of the boat's wooden deck, Pete and Ginny are standing together, leaning against the rail and taking in the excitement of their big day on the water. Unlike several of the other women Ginny is comfortable on board, and eater to get started.

She has her head tucked into Pete's chest, enjoying the comfort of having him near. She is very small, delicately petite, with chin length brown hair and unusually blue eyes.

He had loved this beautiful lady at first sight, and has been totally head over heels for her the last three years. His chest swells with pride for the love they share, and share a private language all their own.

Now he leans down so she can hear his words as he whispers a little nonsense in her ear. She smiles up at him and giggles. He has a great smile, showing lots of perfect white teeth.

Pete said, "I'm glad you felt up to coming on the trip, even though your asthma flared up last night."

"I am, too," she replied, her hand instantly fluttering to her chest. "I'm breathing good right now." She walked to the wood railing of the boat and knocked on it for luck, saying, "Knock on wood," as she did so.

"Ugh, boys, please," whispered Sunny, waving a hand in front of her face only half-jokingly, "you have got to stop that. I thought I was going to have to worry about the bait being smelly, but now that doesn't even bother me."

"Sweetheart," Will replied," that's only all those deviled eggs."

"Just wait," whispered Pete to Ginny, "I had pickled eggs, too!"

Ginny told Sunny, "We may be the 'Jennings' girls, but the boys are the 'Gassey' boys."

As their passengers chatted away, the captain and mate eased in and out of them gracefully, casting off certain lines and securing others, making final preparations for their daylong adventure at sea.

There was no communication system of any kind to shore but this was not uncommon for twelve-year-old vessels, or new ones for that matter. Plans were to travel 30-40 miles out for a day of grouper fishing, and no on e on board expected there to be the slightest hint of trouble.

After all, the forecast for most of the day was clear, and what scattered thunderstorms were predicted for later would occur well after the crew and their passengers were safely back home, sunburned but happy with their catch, reflecting on their day at sea and wishing only it could have lasted an hour or two longer.

Together Captain Wilson and Buck signal a final checklist of last-minute duties, and after securing an errant rod that had come away from its secure spot, Buck signaled his captain that all was ready for their trip.

Nodding, Buck leapt aboard the dock, signaling an impromptu flurry of excitement from the passengers, who realized their trip was about to start. As Captain Wilson fired the engine, sending a great cloud of blue smoke belching from the stern Buck began methodically untying and looping the lines around his arms.

The coils of the weathered rope seemed to fit like sleeves against his shoulders as he strode down the length of the dock, casting off line after line and curling them expertly one after the other.

Already the boat was drifting from the dock and both men and women watched, in awe, as the young deckhand leapt catlike from the dock to land aboard the deck just in time.

Noticing the attention from his passengers, Buck blushed, though it was hard to tell beneath his permanent tan and the shadow produced by the bill of his weathered cap, and grinned to one and all before stowing the ropes where they belonged until they were needed again on the return to Yankeetown.

All stood as the boat easily moved out of the harbor, passing several smaller boats anchored in the shelter of the small local port. Fisherman young and old waved at the Hazy Days as it picked up speed.

Soon enough the fishing boat was cruising past the palm trees and pine scrub dotting the familiar landscape as Buck went to and from securing last minute items that had come loose in the presence of motion and the captain took the wheel, expertly guiding the large vessel through the shallow water and out into deeper sea.

The women instinctively clutched the rail as the boat moved ahead, the morning breeze soon growing stiff against their faces as they clung to their hats with one hand and their mates with he other.

Lois, in particular, was grateful for the brisk air as it masked the true reasons for her shivering, though Bill knew her too well to count her trembling limbs as a result of the stiff breeze.

Pete smiled at Ginny, tugging her closer. Analee found Sam's side, happy to be sheltered in his arms and wearing his pin. Will grasped Sunny, his stomach rumbling as she patted it knowingly, saying, "I told you so," with her eyes if not her lips as she smiled, shaking her head.

Lacey spied out from under her own hat, watching her girlfriends with their husbands, even as her own Lex stood by her side, tall and firm against the rippling tide and splashing water licking at the bow of the Hazy Days.

And so they were twelve plus a crew of two; fourteen carefree souls facing the open waters on a fine Sunday morning in the middle of summer, out for a day of grouper fishing on one of the most popular boats in Yankeetown's modest fleet.

The day dawned clear and right, and was everything they had hoped for. Good friends, close family, easy food and drink just a step away, an able captain and amicable deck hand, both courteous to their guests and capable at their appointed tasks.

Their destiny awaited them, these fourteen brave, unsuspecting souls. Much like the grouper they sought to hook, a cruel fate lurked beneath the crystal blue water just out of reach.

It was hungry, and unforgiving, and cruel.

It was angry and demanding.

It was out there, waiting.

And there wasn't a damn thing any of them could do about it...

CHAPTER 7

Underway

As Buck, the guide, bent to his tasks he smiled broadly to think how much he loved his work. With the wind blowing in his face, the "Hazy Days" cruising along, the fresh dawn of morning winking in his eyes, he couldn't have been happier.

He had lived in the area of Yankeetown all his life. The ropes in his hands and the deck under his feet as familiar and automatic to him as swimming was to the fish he sought to catch later that morning.

His life was good; not a rich life, but a good one. His wife Betty Jo made the best of their modest home, keeping it sparkling clean, and inviting for her husband when he returned home from the sea.

Buck and Captain Wilson were riding high on a long string of chartered fishing runs much like this one. Friendly locals who made the job easy, looking for Buck and the good Captain to provide it for them.

Buck turned from his thoughts of home to the chores at hand, performing them effortlessly and by rote as he smiled from time to time. Occasionally Captain Wilson would give him a signal, instructing him to loosen this gauge or tighten that knot, and together the two work as the passengers at last settled into their "Home away from home" for the next twelve house.

Lacey for one, was making faces more closely resembling Buck's knots than that of a happy sailor. Hailing from Atlanta and considering herself the quintessential "city gal," she knew she could be picky.

"Lex," she complained to her husband as the rest of the passengers settle din amicably amongst themselves, "Why ever did you choose this spot to rest your weary bones?"

"What's wrong with it, dear?" Lex asked good-naturedly, none too eager to ruin a trip he'd waited for with the wrong answer.

She wrinkled her nose even as he tried to avoid rolling his eyes. "Don't you think it's just a tad too close to the motor, darling?"

Lex had to smile, though she'd posed it as a question he knew from experience that it was anything but. Already he was up on his feet, reaching for her hand. "Now that you mention it, honey, you know it sure is. Why don't we just move over here?"

Only after they'd gotten re-settled in a motor noise-free zone of the deck did she at last put on some semblance of a smile. "Now," he asked, as one might a child after drawing them a glass of water in the middle of the night, "isn't that better?"

"I suppose" she replied, though another, more urgent problem soon presented itself. Having moved from the shelter of the deck's central cabin they now found themselves more exposed to the elements.

Lex smiled amicably even as Lacey's pretty, long red hair was kept aloft by the wind, more often than not, began tickling her husband's face. She whined about her hair being "tossed about in the wind," but it was only the beginning of her troubles.

In short order Lacey's scarf was torn from her throat and, turning quickly to catch it her expensive new sunglasses flew from her face and, after a precarious bounce off the rail, fell straight into the water.

"Oh Lex," she whispered, "how ever will I last the day without my sunglasses?

Lex sighed, wishing he could banter and joke with the other fellows gathered on the deck, laughing and enjoying themselves in the sun. "I suppose you'll manage, dear," he said, barely able to keep the tension from his voice.

Lacey might have been spoiled, but she knew her husband's limits. Hearing the strain in his voice, she decided to keep her grousing to a minimum.

For his part, Lex was becoming tired of batting away Lacey's hair from his face. Gathering her hair in his hand, Lex graciously asked if he could push it down her collar and, in that manner, tried to settle her down so at least *one* of them could enjoy the trip. She grudgingly agreed.

The Rosses were not the only ones to be experiencing trouble. After cruising along at a steady speed for most of the morning, the "Hazy Days" suddenly began to show signs of trouble.

A gentle rumble soon rose from the cabin, which had been built around the boat's motor. Though Buck and the Captain had had no trouble starting the engine that morning, they'd been slicing through the choppy waves all morning without incident.

No more; now the motor began to sputter, cutting in and out. The two crew members noticed it immediately, but they weren't alone; the unsettling noises coming from the engine were also causing looks of concern to pass among some of the passengers.

Captain Wilson, sensing their alarm, addressed them personally. "Folks," he said, a strong grin affixed to his suntanned face, "we're just having a little problem with the engine, but don't worry. Everything is going to be all right. Buck and I will get her straightened out in no time."

When neither man moved to address the problem immediately, however, the grumbling continued. "Now, folks, we're just gong to limp a long like this for another mile or two. I want to give the old gal a chance to smooth herself out, but I also want to get a little further out, too an d, if she's still being ornery, we'll stop and take a look at her then."

Lacey looked particularly distressed over the Captain's decision, and tugged at Lex's sleeve so he would ask why. Pete beat him to it, raising a hand on instinct before saying, "Do you really think that's a good idea, Captain?"

The Captain nodded at Pete with an easy grin and explained, "Well, sir that way you fella's can still fish and the ladies can still visit while Buck and I make a few minor adjustments."

Trusting their Captain, the passengers nodded and settled in for a bumpy ride. Some of them, however, were feeling slightly less than settled, through it has less to do with the boat's engine and more to do with their own stomachs.

Sam Pettus was already feeling the unpleasant effects of seasickness.

Sam hung over the side of the boat, feeding the fishes as they say and seriously regretting his decision to have a "big breakfast" to start his "big day."

Between wracking heaves of his breakfast, he watched his jaunty sailor's cap fall into the water and disappear in a wake of his oily stomach contents. In the grim roulette for seasickness, Sam was the day's biggest winner.

Some of the other passengers, the women, mostly, offered pity, others poke a little fun. Bill the Barber, particularly, enjoyed a round of good-natured snickering at the boy's distress.

Sam was too sick too notice, and too pained to care. Long past the point of those painful dry heaves, the college boy was simply moaning as Analee comforted him and murmured reassuring words.

Of course, her own stomach wasn't being helped any by hearing her boyfriend retch into the sea. Already queasy, she tried not to look as Ginny stood next to her, making their side of the boat the designated retching corner.

The women tried to comfort each other with kind words and optimistic sayings, but listening to Sam heave painfully wasn't helping matters any. Between the seasickness and the engine troubles, the two women had plenty to worry about. Sam finally felt well enough to stand erect and wipe his soiled mouth with a trembling hand.

True to his word, the Captain had sailed a few more miles out and was now bringing the boat to a slow course as, beside him, Buck prepared to get down to the business of the day.

Sunny, realizing the deck had suddenly become much less rocky, decided to be helpful and went to the ice box, grabbing a couple of cold cokes. She used the opener hanging from the ice box to open the bottles and then walked first toward Sam.

"Try this, Sam," she said, extending the coke in his direction. "It will help calm your stomach."

Sam looked up and shook his head, waving it away with one hand as he held onto the boat's railing with the other. "No, please I'm sorry, but I don't think I can hold it down. Thanks anyway, Sunny. I really appreciate the thought—"

His words were interrupted by another unexpected wave of nausea and soon Sunny and the rest of the passengers saw what they'd seen most of Sam since the trip began: his back.

Analee looked away, too pained by her boyfriend's discomfort to watch any longer, and noticed Sunny still holding the coke in her outstretched hand. Smiling gratefully, she said, "Sunny, over here, I'll take one."

Sunny nodded in agreement and the girls quickly drank them down. Smiling as the soda's carbonation quickly took effect on their confused stomachs' the women turned to each other and sighed with relief. Slowly, they began inching their way toward the front of the boat to leave Sam to his misery.

Sunny was pleased that she had been able to offer the girl at least some sort of comfort, and quickly moved up the deck toward Will, where a couple of passengers were busy peering over the left side of the boat.

Joining them, Sunny was amazed to discover what they had found: several dolphins that had been off in the distance, but always within eyesight. A pod of dolphins were now right next to the boat, so most of the passengers walked over to see.

It was a nice diversion from both Sam's seasickness and the crew's continued grousing over the confounded engine, which continued to sputter and shake as the two shipmates tended to it with equal parts confidence and unease.

Ginny and Sunny, in particular, were both talking to the dolphins and encouraging the others to "come and take a look!"

Lex's wife, Lacey, took one look and offered: "Those creatures look decidedly slimy, and I, for one, do not want to have anything to do with them." Lex watched forlornly as she turned from the good-natured sea creatures and ambled off to find a breezy spot.

Sighing, he turned to join her...

Lois, who had been dead-set against the trip at first was beginning to feel a little more comfortable, and for her part, was enchanted by the dolphins.

"Look Lois," urged Ginny as she quickly joined them. "They're so smart, they know we're talking to them."

"Do you think they know what we're saying?" Lois asked Sunny.

Sunny smiled back. "There's only one way to find out!" She replied.

Lois took Sunny at her word, trying the hardest among all the passengers to get a reaction from the frolicking sea creatures. Watching their gray, thick skin shining in the bright morning sun, she "chattered" back and forth, doing her best to mimic their nautical language.

Amazingly, it worked; the dolphins chattered back nodding their head up and down and splashing with delight. Periodically they broke contact to disappear beneath the water momentarily, only to emerge seconds later in a burst of salt spray and squeaks to leap over each other before returning to "talk" to Lois. Everyone was having fun watching them and Lois, in particular, was suddenly glad Bill "dragged" her along.

Hank watched the dolphin show like everybody else, but couldn't help wondering what was gong on in the cabin. He was not a superstitious man, nor a pessimistic one. But he was realistic. While he entertained no thoughts of doom and gloom, he *was* concerned that the sputtering engine could ruin their day at sea, or at least shorten it, and wanted to prevent it if at all possible.

"What seems to be the problem, boys?" he asked as he entered the close quarters of the cabin to find Buck and the Captain hunched over the engine, looking puzzled but no overly concerned. Bill came in and climbed in a bunk, leaning over to advise.

"Damned if I know," murmured the Captain, looking up without his usual grin.

"Well," Hank offered, bending down to peer at the engine, "maybe I can be of some help."

"Don't mind if you do," said Buck, once more, they bent to see if they could figure out what might be wrong with the Hazy Day's twelve-year-old engine.

Out on deck, Will suddenly felt parched and asked Sunny for a soda and a ham sandwich. Sunny tossed the sandwich to him, but in a joking mood Pete leaned over with surprising dexterity and effortlessly grabbed the sandwich out of the air.

"Hungry Will?" he teased as he held the tempting sandwich up in the air.

"Why you little cuss," Will laughed, good-naturedly playing along as he attempted to snatch the sandwich back.

Pete decided to play a quick game of "keep away" with it, and teased Will mercilessly, pretending to gobble down the sandwich as the two men danced around the open deck like little boys, making the most of their day at sea.

Smiling at their carefree antics, Ginny asked for a soda as well. Seeing the "Gassey" boys horsing around, she decided to join them and enjoy the fun. As the trio flitted effortlessly from toe to toe, Will narrowly missing the sandwich time and time again, the dolphins chatted just off the boat's stern, their endless squeaking competing over the sounds of the wheezing engine.

The happy scene was, in fact, the calm before the storm...

CHAPTER 8

❁

Explosion at Sea

Captain Wilson, Buck, and Hank were crowded in the cabin when the engine stopped completely. One minute it sputtered, as it had all morning, and the next it stalled, shaking the tiny berth with this rattling death knell.

Puzzled, the mechanical trio shook their heads in unison, cocking a quizzical eye at one another before cursing the engine in low voices so the women just outside the cabin wouldn't hear.

The breakdown was bittersweet; for one thing, it meant the worst had come true for the crew and their guests, and yet for another the ceasing of the rattling would mean less heat in the brutally oppressive cabin. For the men gathered around the blasted contraption, however, it meant little more than a leap from the frying pan into the fire.

The three men huddled close nonetheless, tools in hand, trying to identify the source of the problem. There were plenty of leads to follow, but one by one they all resulted in dead ends. Bill in the bunk beside them suggested checking the plugs, which they did.

In short order the men agreed that the plugs were in good shape, the bearings in order, and that no saltwater had found its way in to gum up the works.

He sat up in his bunk and continued to offer his advice, whether they needed it or not. Looking down from his perch on high, he was not surprised that the three men hunched over the engine ignored him' they obviously had their hands full as they tapped gauges and eyeballed various gears to see if, perhaps, one had somehow run afoul.

Sweat crept down their backs, staining their shirts with grimy, inverted triangles that crept from the napes of their necks toward the smalls of their backs as they toiled with gears and gizmos to isolate the engine's malfunction.

Lex, perhaps eager to see if he could help the stalled engine, poked his head in the doorway to see if he might be of some assistance. It didn't really matter if he could help or not; he just wanted a moment's diversion and was bound and determined to get it.

"What seems to be the problem, fellas?" he asked innocently, soon to learn what Bill already had: this was neither the time, nor the place, for idle chitchat. He and Bill exchanged questioning glances, but got none in reply.

Not having dropped anchor because they were not quite to the fishing grounds yet, both Captain Wilson and Buck realized they were drifting aimlessly at sea, but neither man could find the time to remedy the situation just yet.

It was a moot point, they knew: this far out at sea there was nothing to bump into but, both men realized in humorless irony, just as little to grab onto. If they couldn't get the boat started again, they were indeed stranded. The pressure mounted in their pounding chests as they struggled to get the engine restarted.

Even so the men were cautiously optimistic; they'd been here before, and always battled back to fight—and fish—another day. Truth be told, boats and breakdowns went together like fish and bait, or landlubbers and seasickness. They were used to the minor malfunction; their passengers weren't. Bill and Lex tried to be patient but after being ignored long enough, Bill at last reiterated his question.

Trying to be pleasant, Buck flashed an inconsequential smile and blurted, almost by rote, "There seems to be some fuel leakage here, fellas. The Captain and I are trying to fix it but as you can see we're not having much luck yet—"

Almost on cue, Captain Wilson began cinching off a leaky fuel valve with his handy pair of needle-nose pliers. Buck noticed the pinchers still bore fish guts from the last time they'd used them getting the hook out of a grouper's throat!

Having placated his male onlookers, at least in theory, Buck bent back to the engine, his own tool in hand. In this case it was a socket wrench that ratcheted and clicked as he worked to tighten up the bolts that housed the engine casing.

Perhaps the fuel was coming from there, he thought idly, and though he and the Captain both doubted it they knew doing something about their plight was a lot better than doing nothing. Perhaps cutting the leak off at the source would save some of the strain on the boat's tired old hoses.

Unfortunately, the oil leak had affected both men's hands. The slick motor oil mixed with the men's perspiration made their purchase on the tools of choice tenuous at best, and at last a tool was dropped.

Instinctively both the Captain and his mate reached for it, realizing a spark from metal hitting metal could ignite the leaking fuel and blow them all to smithereens before it ever touched the ground. Their shoulders clashed, their heads butted, their breath caught as the two adult males slammed into the same spot at the same time. Buck was able to push back rather quickly and try again to catch the tool.

Too late; the tool avoided their reach and clanged against the metal engine casing, ricocheting from one metal surface to the other and at last emitting just what both men feared: a rain of sparks that disappeared into the engine with a glowing red menace that spelled disaster.

For the men in the tight-spaced cabin, time slowed to a standstill, then stopped altogether. Mouths agape, hands outstretched, sweat dripping from their trembling noses, there was nothing for any of them to do now but wait for the inevitable.

But not for long: the rain of sparks ignited the displaced engine oil—much more had leaked than both men dared to suspect—resulting in a gigantic fire-ball that rushed from the engine housing as if propelled from hell itself. Up and out it came, a roaring billow of flame that roared from the darkness and screamed through the cabin, licking everything in its path.

The vacuum from the energy the fireball so greedily consumed sucked the room of air for but a second, maybe even less, and only the two experienced seafarers realized its implications.

It was like the saltwater that gets sucked from the beach in advance of an approaching wave; one minute it was there, the next it was gone. It mattered little; in no time the raging ball of fire engulfed Captain Wilson like a human marshmallow roasted on a stick.

Too fast to feel the pain, he nonetheless knew it was coming as the slick stench of seared flesh assaulted his nostrils like a living thing. Even in breathing he could not escape the flames; the sudden intake of breath invited the fire in, singing off every nose hair and cauterizing the roof of his mouth. Instinctively he raced from the cabin and leapt overboard into the salty brine, desperate to escape the inferno that licked at his chest, legs and back, completely aflame.

The fireball pursued the Captain, doggedly searching for release, searing Hank like a flank steak and setting his shirt on fire as it belched forth from the cabin, feeding on the oxygen on deck and flashing past—and through—the passengers mingling innocently on board before they had a chance to react.

Lex, who had been standing in the doorway, was blown back by the explosion but could not escape its effects: much of his face was badly burned, he inhaled with the shock of the impact, his lungs were seared by the blast.

People screamed, and ran, and pushed each other, acting on impulse and immediately scrambling to avoid the hissing orange ball of fire and reacting on sheer animal instinct, succumbing to the fight or flight mechanism that had made it possible for them to survive.

The sounds of the speeding explosion—it seemed to be a living thing, following some doggedly and ignoring others whimsically—was unlike anything any of them had ever heard before; a great rushing hiss that screamed in their ears even as it sucked the oxygen from their very lungs.

The heat from the flames was oppressive; even those not directly in the blast zone felt it singe their eyebrows and hair, making their throats dry and eyes water as the furnace blast erupted all around them, threatening to engulf them all before it was at last extinguished. Sunny, ever the hostess, had been in the process of turning around to get more sodas from the cooler when the blast erupted. She'd been enjoying the friendly game of "keep away" and turned but for a second when the force of the blast knocked her roughly to the deck, as if an unseen hand had shoved her with such force it laid her out flat.

Splinters from the weathered wood surface bit into her knees and the palms of her trembling hands, but that was the least of her worries; one side of her hair was suddenly on fire!

Seeing the small blaze threatening to engulf his wife's entire head, Will rushed over to help her, dropping the sandwich. He smothered the fire with his fishing cap and managed to put it out while Sunny remained motionless; drained by shock, unable to rise.

He put his arms around her and held tight; feeling her heart pounding rapidly against her chest even as the heat and smoke from her smoldering hair assaulted his nostrils, he just thanked God she was alive.

Sunny was not alone in her fight with the voracious fireball. Hank, who had been close to the engine room, emerged with his shirt on fire, floundering wildly like a madman and scrambling from one side of the deck to the other, panic overtaking him.

Flames licked at his buttons, swallowed his collar, and threatened to leap from fabric to skin. Before he could follow Captain Wilson's lead and dive from the boat, however, a quick-thinking Sam and Analee managed to grab him and beat out the flames on his shirt.

It was no easy feat; their hands stung like hornets from the fire but they had no other tools at their disposal and no hesitation when it came to saving their friend. Hank needed their help and they provided it, realizing only to late the pain it might produce.

They ignored it, and beat on…

Amazingly, though he was in the cabin when the explosion occurred, Bill's perch on the upper berth had kept him fairly safe from the blast. Though his face was red with heat and every pore in his body burst forth a slick sheen of oily perspiration, he was otherwise unhurt.

His ears would ring for the next few minutes, but considering the alternative he knew this was a small price to pay for avoiding the kinds of burns he knew the others had just received.

If anything, he seemed to be the sole voice of reason on deck. He reacted with a lightning speed; picking up all the lifejackets he could carry as he rushed out of the cabin as he yelled for both Pete and Will to help him.

Pete, who had been lingering around the cabin and was nearly bowled over by Bill in his haste to emerge from the tiny room, had seen what the others had not. He wondered whether or not he should share the grim news he alone had spotted, and knew instinctively that by avoiding the truth he was only delaying the inevitable.

Clearing his throat, Pete said, "I have some really bad news, guys; the explosion blew a big hole in the bottom of the boat. I can hear sea water rushing in; it's already flooding through the bottom of the cabin floor.

He paused, cleared his throat, and looked at his bewildered shipmates before continuing his dire announcement: "This boat is going to sink soon, and we don't want to be on it when it does."

Not surprisingly, the announcement sent a wave of shock through the group. The women clung to each other, desperate in their fear and eager for comfort of any sort. It was like a bad dream.

When would they wake up?

The passengers retreating into a world of shock and pain, some reacting with a dread sense of calm that allowed them to think rationally despite the grim predicament they'd somehow found themselves in.

After a tense minute of heated discussions and opinions one thing became painfully clear: arguing was getting them nowhere. Only action, it seemed, would solve the problem.

Buck was burned on his left arm and shoulder and now was frantically leaned over the boat's weathered railing in search of his Captain, the conversation fell to the inadequate number of life jackets Bill had managed to retrieve from the still smoldering cabin.

They were moldy affairs, canvas vest with strips of cork in small pockets on the front of the vest, long strings to tie at neck and the long strings that tied at the waist. There was not enough; of the fourteen passengers and crew less than half that many would have the luxury of one of the life jackets.

It wasn't hard to do the math: after a hurried discussion, the men decided to put the few life jackets on the women. At least all six of them could wear one and that, at least, brought the men some small comfort.

Few thought to blame the Captain and Buck for the accident. For one it was no use crying over spilt milk and for another it wasn't entirely their fault. As yet there was no law requiring a set number of life jackets per passenger, and certainly not one that required one jacket per passenger.

The women protested, of course. Ginny even went so far as to suggest that if everybody couldn't have one, no one could. But even she saw the shortsightedness of that rash suggestion and quietly succumbed to her husband's instructions as he fussed with her jacket, pulling the canvas over her head and tying the strings to which the vest was affixed around her waist.

Sparks, flames, and smoke still surged from the cabin as the lifejackets were dispersed. Only minutes had passed since the explosion, and survival was uppermost on everyone's mind. Thinking only to protect Ginny from more fire, Pete had taken her shirt off and before anyone could protest, least of all poor Ginny, quickly tossed it overboard.

In pain from the burns, and only looking to help, Lex was quick to do the same with Lacey's shirt. Other men were eager to follow, and reached to remove their wives' tops, but just as Lacey's blouse hit the water, however, Buck realized what was happening and yelled, "Keep your shirts on you guys, trust me, you'll need them to protect you from the sun."

Ginny and Lacey looked longingly after their drifting clothes. A feeling of dread and foreboding sunk into their bare stomachs, and instinctively they covered themselves even as they peered overboard at the drowning fabric.

"What was I thinking! I can't believe I threw your shirt overboard," Pete lamented to Ginny, already picturing her skin blistering in the sun.

She just stared at her shirt as it slowly sank. It floated for a moment, its bright color contrasting with the film of oil that had already suffused the water's surface, until at last it succumbed and sank slowly into the briny depths.

"That's all right, Pete, you were only trying to help."

Lex was hardly able to think. The pain was really bad. He didn't want Lacey to know how bad it was.

CHAPTER 9

Into the Sea

Buck straddled the rail and leaned over the bow, torn between searching for his missing Captain and helping the passengers prepare to abandon ship. Despite his many years of training, Buck blanched midway through his search, recalling in his mind's eye the last sight he'd seen of his friend before he dove overboard: one hand burned beyond recognition, on fire, and one thumb burned to the bone, resembling more the point of a pencil than a human appendage. Seeing his friend in such shape, Buck struggled to regain control of his emotions, not to mention his stomach, and now he was somehow in charge.

Perhaps, he reasoned, the Captain was better off where he was...

Realizing Captain Wilson was no longer for this world, Buck turned to the passengers, who still were—and looked a fright. Many were clutching their hands protectively, some of which had been singed putting out their family or friends or touching surfaces still smoldering and much hotter than they looked.

Ginny and Lacey were shirtless, their thin arms trembling from shock and panic as they hugged their arms. Normally Buck would have blushed at such a strange sight, but this was no time for modesty or other such everyday concerns.

Buck knew time was of the essence. Behind the passengers, clustered haphazardly in groups of two or three, the cabin hissed with licking flames even as the unsteady craft began listing to one side as water flooded the ravaged hold and spilled over the ship's hull. Instinct took over at last. "Everyone?" Buck asked, but the clear tone in his thick, husky voice made it clear that this was no question. Quickly the men and women quieted, turning to stare at the young man at the back of the boat.

I'm sure this is unbelievable," he began firmly, eager not to feed them too much too soon. "This is something none of us expected, but now that it's happened, there's no denying its seriousness."

Licking his lips to quell his nervousness, he continued bravely on, "I know this must look like the worst thing ever happened to you but, if you follow my lead, I can help you through this and, together, we can all be home having dinner tonight."

Not giving the group time to doubt him, he said, "We're going to have to work together. That means everyone. The worst thing that could happen right now is to have too many cooks in the kitchen."

Even through his fear and the concern for his trembling wife, Lois, that gripped at his very soul, Bill managed to quip, "Guess that makes you our chef, huh son?"

Frightened laughter greeted the remark, which Buck encouraged, anything to keep their minds off the inevitable.

"That's right, sir," he responded politely. "And as your chef I've got a recipe for survival. I need you to listen to what I have to say…Ladies; it's time to quit fussing about your louses. We need you to finish getting those life jackets on and on quick.

"Men? I know I told you not to get rid of anybody's shirts but your pants will have to go. They'll be waterlogged in no time and there's no telling how long we'll be in the water. They'll just slow you down and, what's worse, weigh you down."

Buck waited for the group to comply, searching their eyes to see if any of them had registered his remark about how long they'd be in the water, from the looks of it, apparently not.

Eager to comply, the men all stripped to their underwear in order to be lighter in the water, kicked off their shoes, and gave their wallets to their wives. Some of the women had purses and they hung onto them desperately, clinging to any sense of normalcy they might sill provide in the wake of this sudden disaster. Into the purses went the wallets.

Only Sunny, obviously in shock and blistered by the fire was having a hard time untying the sash on her sundress, so she put the vest right over he dress.

By now the sound of gurgling could be heard coming from the engine room, and even if it hadn't it was clear by sight alone that the boat was sinking more quickly, as the rest of the passengers scrambled on the deck, untying their shoes and pulling off their pants.

At last it all becomes too much. Lois, who'd been silent throughout the ordeal, perhaps as much from shock as disbelief, now became terrified as she realized she would have to get in the water. She alternated between crying pitifully and screaming violently.

She who had only fished from the shore until today was now preparing to go into the water. And not just any water, but the ocean depths. Desperately terrified of deep water, Lois realized as well as anybody that now they were going in where it was very, every deep. Her panic galvanized the group. They circled around her. Sunny and Ginny, sisters that loved the water, said, "Lois, it's really only for a little while, we will be rescued very soon." They were both trying to assist her. Kate and Lacey were unable to assist because the injuries to their husbands had them in a state of disbelief. Trying to comfort Lois as best he could, Bill helped her take off her shoes and put on one of the flimsy life jackets.

The outburst passed, but everyone knew the terror in Lois's eyes meant it would return eventually. Perhaps, by then, they would have all joined her. For now, though, they set about doing as they were told.

One by one, the men assisted the ladies into the life jackets and told them they had to jump, but none did. It was a sudden stalemate; they just stood there, staring at the endless sea, perhaps imagining their Captain's burned and blackened body bobbing just below the surface like a listless cork and seeing their future writ large upon his pained and melted features.

Lois trembled, inching away from the side of the boat even as bill guided her gently back. The other women were no more eager to leave the deck; putting the life jackets on was one thing, volunteering to jump was quite another.

Ginny and Pete whispered to each other, solving their problems as always, alone and in private. Sam Pettus was surprised that Analee should be so hesitant to leap into the water. He knew of her background at Silver Springs and thought for sure the leap would be a snap.

But one look at her trembling shoulders and he knew he was wrong. This was no summer job; this was life or death.

Looking at the frightened women, each man realized what he had to do. They shared a unanimous look of concern, which soon passed into resolve. Sam was first to move, whether out of genuine concern for Analee or the welfare of the entire group it mattered little.

He placed his hand firmly in the small of her long, slender back. Feeling her flinch, he whispered in her ear, "Leesie, we must do this to survive. The boat is sinking; there's nothing else we can do. Don't worry, I'll be with you. I'm right behind you."

"No," she said, quickly qualifying it by adding, "I want you beside me. We can go in together."

Sam smiled; a victory was a victory.

As he moved closer to the edge of the deck, he watched as Analee hesitate, looking at the lifejacket in her hand. He sensed she was making a decision—he'd seen that look before—and she quickly slipped out of her colorful blouse before slipping it on.

Sam whispered, "didn't you hear what Buck said? You'll need that to keep the sun off."

Analee bit her lip as she explained, "I know, Sam, but think about it; once we're in the water there won't be a chance to get out of this life jacket. We might be able to use the blouse, to signal a rescue boat or to cover our heads, switch back and forth somehow. But if I wear it under my vest, there won't be any chance of that, now will there?"

She was always a step or two ahead of him. If anyone could survive this ordeal, it was Analee Morgan. And because of her, he might just survive as well.

"Good thinking," he whispered.

Together the two edged over the back of the boat, their hands desperately clinging to each other as they ignored the splinters in the wood and sipped effortlessly into the briny deep.

The water was jarring, and surprisingly cold. Analee, an expert swimmer, nonetheless sputtered and splashed. Sam righted himself quickly, and adjusted her life jacket, which had somehow become bunched at her neck. She spat salt-water from her mouth, helped him, and together the two turned to face the rest of their group.

The move seemed to galvanize those left on deck. One by one the couples descended into the choppy water. Ginny clung desperately to Pete until at last she was over and only then did he join her, holding onto her shoulders.

Bill was glad Lois's outburst was over as he helped her into the water. Even so he watched her features carefully, realizing she could swing from shock to panic in the blink of an eye, and hoping against hope that she could keep it together long enough for him to join her.

When he did, he breathed a sigh of relief. Only then did he realize the irony of the situation: here she was, bobbing to and fro on the open water, and yet he was relieved to no longer be on the deck of a sinking ship.

For once, he kept his silent laughter to himself…

When it was clear they were incapable of doing so themselves, Buck assisted the injured Hank and his wife, Kate into the water. It was no easy feat; Hank was badly burned on his chest, arms, and face.

His eyebrows were singed off, giving his face a ghoulish appearance, and his hair was burned; it lay matted and stiff where the fireball had seared it to hank's very scalp.

He was suffering from shock, which was keeping him oblivious to the blinding pain that would surely follow nonetheless found him helpless to do anything more than stay afloat.

He bobbed up and down in the water, kicking and flailing out of sheer instinct as his wife tried to steady him. Kate was tougher than she looked and to see Hank so badly burned made her only more resolved to get them through this ordeal and fin d him the best medical help available once they returned to Ocala.

Will and Sunny went in with hardly a splash. Last to go overboard were Lacey and Lex. Lex was also badly burned and in shock, and no help to his panicky wife. Buck took her jacket and helped her into it.

He righted her life jacket and "Helped" her overboard with a little push. She hit the water with a small splash.

Buck was more careful with Lex, whose skin was now blistering and warm to the touch. Lex groaned with insufferable pain as Buck lowered him into the water, and though he felt horrible for the man's condition, Buck knew there was no other way but to manhandle him into the water. Lacey was in sheer panic calling softly her husbands name. In any event, Buck counted heads as he viewed the bobbing figures of his passengers in the water.

He felt the clutches of panic grip his belly as he realized they were counting on him to rescue them. Without his captain, Buck felt lost, as adrift at sea in the depths of his mind as were his passengers bobbing atop the growing waves.

Seeing the future and trying desperately to prevent it, Buck found a rope from the wreckage and threw it into the water. As he did so he struggled to shout over the now powerfully gurgling water threatening to swallow the "Hazy Days."

"Okay everyone!" he said. "Everyone, get a good grip on the rope. It's important that we all stay together. There is safety in numbers; this rope will help us do that. No matter what, hold onto the rope."

He watched as the group followed his lead, sloshing through the water to take hold of the rope. It inspired him to see that not only could the group follow instructions, but they instinctively coiled the rope until they were closest together, allowing the slack to trail out behind them instead of letting it keep them apart.

By now Buck was knee-deep in water as the sea threatened to swallow the boat any minute. He struggled frantically to find anything that might help them survive what was sure to be a life or death struggle, but by now what hadn't been destroyed immediately in the fire was either water-logged and sinking or had already floated away.

Among those items that floated listlessly in the debris aboard the water on deck was Will's uneaten sandwich, a meal he would soon wish for in the many hours stretching before him, especially since he was the only one on board who'd neglected to eat breakfast.

There were also several broken but untouched Cokes that bled their bubbly brown liquid into the sea instead of quenching the thirsts of those who had clutched them only moments before the explosion.

Buck ignored the waterlogged slices of bread and bobbing soda bottles as he sloshed frantically from one side of the deck to the other. He'd crewed aboard the "Hazy Days" for six months but gave nary a backward glance as he dove headfirst into the ocean. Without a life jacket, he began dog-paddling immediately, his strong, long legs beating a rhythmic pattern into which he soon settled.

He knew energy was a commodity, and that the longer they could stay afloat the better their chance of rescue. He saw the other men, most of them inexperienced swimmers, kicking and thrashing wildly, half-clinging to the rope half-struggling with buoyancy, and knew he would have to remind them to conserve energy sooner rather than later.

The group held tight to the rope, glad to be together and, for the moment, proud of their resolve to enter the sea and not look back. The water was a little choppy, filling their mouths with the occasional splash of seawater, but they could still see the faithful dolphins, who were so playful just moments before, still circling close by, almost warily, protectively.

"Start moving away from the boat," Buck called as they hovered just off the bow. "I know the boat seems like security by now, but it will sink very soon and as it goes down whatever's closest could get sucked down with it."

The group reacted as one, paddling away from the boat and dragging those who are just hanging onto the rope along with it. "Okay." Buck shouted when they were far enough away from the "Hazy Days" for him to feel more comfortable, though far from safe. "This is far enough."

He waited until he had the group's full attention before he continued, "We're all going to need our energy, and no one can do it all by him- or herself. Put the burned men in the middle, where everyone can take turns helping them. It's the best way for us to stay together and save our energy."

The other men, somewhat abashed at not having come up with the idea themselves, complied willingly, eagerly taking Lex and Hank off their wife's hands and putting them in the middle of the group.

No longer forced to care for Hank, at least for the time being, Kate watched as Pete helped him remain afloat. When he had been behind her, she had been unable to see the full extent of his burns. Now she was crying stunned into disbelief to see her husband so badly burned.

For his part, Hank drifted in and out of consciousness. Though he had managed to keep the lid on his emotions to this point, he was not sure how long he could remain strong.

Though the others didn't realize it, he had not mentioned it, struggling through his pain and shock to form any words at all, the salt water was vicious to his burns.

They were bad enough on their own, and perhaps even manageable aboard the boat. But now each lap of water threatened to send him closer and closer to madness. Each burn sang out in pain and discomfort as the water kissed his seared flesh, sending the damaged nerve ending screaming with a white-hot pain that felt like enduring the fireball all over again.

Lex's lips were bleeding from biting on them during each wave of pain, and now the nausea from bouncing up and down and fighting the constant savagery of his wounds as threatening to overtake him.

Lacey fought back tears as she witnessed her husband's eyes roll into the back of his head one more time. The pain was evident, even if nobody else saw it. What would she do without him? She needed him more than ever, but now it was he who needed her.

Guiltily, she admitted to herself that she might not be up to the task. She knew she could often be vain, and petty, and a tad self-centered, but wasn't it Lex who spoiled her into believing she was special enough to get away with it?

Now the light of her life was slowly going out; retreating into himself from the power of his pain before her very eyes. She watched as Barber Bill bided his time between his own frightened wife, Lois, and her husband, Lex.

She clung tightly to the rope, avoiding the eyes of the rest of the group and fearing for their safety. Lex was so strong. If he could be weakened to the point of insanity by a rogue fireball on a sunny Sunday afternoon, what hope did any of the rest of them have?

Buck eyed the group, for any of them to survive they must remain calm and not panic, and he knew they had been idle too long.

He looked for a diversion, something to keep them occupied. He could always give them another speech, but he feared they were tired of being lectured and was afraid it was all too much, too soon for the struggling group of thirteen to handle.

He was relieved to spot a mattress from the wrecked cabin bobbling atop a series of slowly forming white caps.

"Ahoy there," he cried, if only to lighten the mood just a tad. "See that bunk mattress just out of reach? Let's all swim together and grab it. It looks big enough for us all to hold onto and perhaps it will give our legs a break."

The group became inspired, as they all kicked and splashed to reach the bunk-size mattress. He helped them open up one end of the rope to close in the mattress, and though it was not wide it was quite long and, spreading out along its rectangular sides, the group of thirteen held on for as long as they could.

It turned out to be a brief respite; after only a few hours the mattress became waterlogged and was becoming more of a load than a floatation device. Reluctantly, they let it go and watched as it drifted away along a wave before it disappeared into the darkening depths.

The group watched it drown silently, the unspoken message loud and clear among the thirteen adults who were no doubt thinking the exact same thing: Will I suffer the same fate this day?

Some struggled valiantly to remain optimistic; shooing the thought. Others resigned themselves to the inevitable and found it hard to go on.

Through it all Buck was their cheerleader, urging them on, stressing the importance of staying together, reminding them to conserve their energy and kick only hard enough to stay afloat.

Time passed and the group fell into an unsteady rhythm. Bursts of energy seemed to pass through them spontaneously, and then retreat as quickly as they'd formed.

Since the rope was the only thing keeping them together, they decided to also tie the jackets together. The jackets had 18-20 inch lines on the vests. It was far from the best solution, but it was the only thing they had to help them float, and together.

Soon even the rope became sodden and heavy with water, and they reluctantly let it go, realizing to that their only lifeline to each other was disappearing.

The men had no choice, but to cling to the women. This pulled the women further under the waterline, causing them to choke.

Buck watched the events unfold helplessly. Already the group was a bright pink, exhausted, panicked, and sputtering for life. He eyed the sun, shaking his head as he marked its slow, inevitable progress overhead.

They'd had been in the water less than six hours…

CHAPTER 10

Waterlogged

"I'm so thirsty! So terribly, terribly thirsty! And why?!? How could you not remember to grab some Cokes before you made me jump!"

The complaints were coming from none other than Lacey Ross. The only benefit from the searing pain and singed eardrums resulting from his third-degree burns was that her poor husband, Lex, couldn't hear them.

Unfortunately, the rest of the survivors could.

Even so, most of them were too bogged down with their own woes to do much about it. Analee, the youngest and strongest of the women, whispered to her boyfriend Sam to "stop her" but without the aid of a life jacket he was having enough of a struggle just keeping his head above water.

The hours in the water had taken their toll; sprits were listless and drained; hope was dwindling fast. Even the beautiful and impish Analee looked like a different person; strands of wet, salty hair hung to her forehead even as her sunburned nose shined very red.

Whatever attempts she'd made at applying makeup that morning were long since gone; now the elements had stripped her, stripped them all, to the most base and elemental. She was all legs and arms, kicking relentlessly, splashing little, using every bit of instinct and training she'd ever received at the amusement park to stay alive.

Like a barnacle, Sam clung to her, trying his best to lessen his weight so as not to be a burden, but failing from time to time and hearing a soft, quiet grunt as her only form of protest.

For his part, Will had tried to lighten the spirit of the group by teasing Pete about still being "gassey," croaking out something about "water bubbles" and "noxious fumes," but the joke had since grown as sodden and waterlogged as the survivors and was no longer funny.

Meanwhile, Lacey was continuing to rant and rave. Her voice seemed to rise and fall with the lapping of the waves, it crested then fell, at once shrill and demanding and yet equally faint and distant, until eventually her own weariness did what the complaining of the others could not: silenced her at last.

Lex tried to drown out more than just his wife, but indeed the pain that coursed through every inch of his scarred and blistered body. Each wave of lukewarm salt water caused his pain to renew; meanwhile the noonday sun beat down on them all, slathering his already oozing wounds with a fresh dose of blinding pain as the damaging ultraviolet rays took up where the engine fire had left off.

He countered the effects of Mother Nature with those of Father Time and tried in vain to travel back to an earlier day, when life was little more than the endless rows of shoes back at the Family Shoe Store and a series of mornings and evenings that ran together into a not unpleasant life for he and Lacey.

Despite his pain he forgave her for her apparent anger, recognizing it for the fear it really was. He saw the faces of the other survivors, heard their groans of protests and whispered pleas to "make her stop."

He alone knew the secret Lackey, the kind Lacey, the caring Lacey, and realized that it was only abject terror causing her to say such awful words to the wounded man clinging to her back.

Even that shamed him; to be floating, bobbing and helpless; clinging like a barnacle to his wife's back was the ultimate insult. If it weren't for the pain he might have cursed out loud.

Instead he groaned, and clenched his teeth in advance of yet another wave as the sea pushed and pulled at them, roughly urging the close-knit group where it wanted them to go and then yanking them back rudely as if it had just changed its mind.

In the wake of Lacey's silence, the other couples began murmuring amongst themselves. The rope that had bound them together during the earliest hours had long since disappeared along with their tackle, their gear, their boat and worst of all, their supplies.

Bound together by the fragile life jackets, the group clung tightly to each other. From time to time a large wave or strange current would tug at one of the survivors or another, threatening to tear them apart, but instinctively the nearest person would drag the hapless wanderer back into the group.

Buck's words as he had urged them all into the sea, "We've GOT to stay together in order to survive," became their unspoken mantra. They might not have had much at this point, but at least they still had each other.

Bu no, that wasn't entirely true: silently the survivors mourned their fallen comrade, Captain L. B. Wilson. Only 34, he left behind a wife and three kids, the latest to be widowed and left fatherless by the sea.

Each prayed for his safe return to the ultimate fisher of men as the day dragged on. Though his name was little spoken, his memory was honored as lips silently moved and eyes closed reverently, not in protest to the blistering sun but to honor the dead and mourn his passing, and to ask for their own survival.

Perhaps, too, the brave men and women left battling the sea wondered if the Captain's fate could soon be their own. He had seemed so strong and solid. A weathered seaman, how could they survive where he had not?

The group especially eyed Lex and Hank, both burned savagely and suffering terribly. How long, they wondered silently, could they last? The sheer agony of their ordeal was painted all over their melted, mottled faces.

Could they endure the passing hours, the blinding sun, the singing salt that suffused the ocean water and made its cooling waves a double-edged sword? Of course, the two burn victims were not alone in their suffering.

By now more hours had passed and the group was sweltering under the afternoon sun. It beat down upon them mercilessly, filling the cloudless blue sky as exposure to the elements quickly grew from annoyance to discomfort to agony.

It was the extremities that took the highest toll; the crowns of their heads burned raw and exposed, their shoulders glowed a savage red, their noses cried out for relief; yet there was none to be found.

They drifted aimlessly, at the mercy of the elements, the sea, the sun, the endless hours that stretched before them. They had no food, no water, no supplies, nothing but the half-dozen ragged lifejackets and each other.

Pete and Ginny were on one end of the circular group. They clung to each other, whispering words of encouragement when one or the other suffered a leg cramp from their endless dog-paddling or their voice cracked from the emotion, fear, and dread of their predicament.

"Petey," he whispered gently in Ginny's ear. "I know I'm too heavy for you; I'd like to let go, give you more chance of survival."

She reached from the water and clung tightly to his forearm.

"Don't you dare!" she spat fiercely. "Don't you dare leave me alone in this world; I'll never make it without you. I'm not weaker because you're on my back; I'm stronger. Didn't anybody tell you 'two heads are better than one'?"

He smiled grimly.

Bill and Lois Saunders clung just as desperately to each other in the middle of the pack. She who was so afraid to be on open water was now surrounded by it; but her abject fear had been replaced by the desire to survive.

Bill mumbled apologies in her ear; he was sorry for dragging her out here, sorry for not listening, sorry for this, sorry for that, but she shushed him with the annoyed air of a mother shooing her children from the cookie dough.

"I'm just as to blame for letting you talk me into this Bill Saunders," she replied to his murmurings, almost as much to herself as to her husband. "What's done is done; you've said it yourself a million times, 'Once a hair is cut, there's no way to get it back on the customer's head.' All we can do is help each other through this."

She expected a joke in reply, but all she heard was his sigh of guilt and continued murmurings. Had their roles reversed? She wondered as they clung to each other. Was she now the strong one, trying to lighten his load with humor as he had done so effectively with her over the years?

She had little time to ponder the bigger questions; out of nowhere a whitecap rocked them where they floated at the end of jacket strings, threatening to send them from the group until Sam, rousing himself from Analee's back, reached out to grab them both and reel them back in.

"It's almost like fishing," he quipped to no one in particular.

Beside him, Lex groaned in continued pain while Lacey murmured to herself. Sunny and Will floated nearby, as they grew lost in their own thoughts, Will wondering idly if he'd ever get behind the wheel of a big rig again and she fearing for the future of their three children were they not to survive the ordeal.

Rounding out the circle of friends and family were Kate and Hank Mays. Like Lacey, Kate suffered alone with her badly burned husband. He clung listlessly to her aching back, his breath coming in short, broken rasps as his singed esophagus tried in vain to feed his brain oxygen.

Each wheeze that passed across his swollen lips was pure agony, and accompanied by a sickening, sound that had Kate dreading the sound as much as she was reassured by it.

The ravages of the engine fire had reduced her poor husband to a survival state; he had not uttered a word since they'd been plunged into the ocean and she feared he might never again.

His body existed on pure impulse; miraculously he managed to move his legs back and forth in the water, falling into a rhythm with hers as if on auto-pilot. Even so, she could tell he'd weakened in the last few hours and minute by minute his sunburnt arms grew heavy on her sore, tired shoulders.

In concert with her husband's ragged wheezing the water lapped at her chin, each wave threatened to fill her mouth with salt water, as the weight of her husband grew greater and greater with each passing hour.

Panic raged inside her shrieking mind as she wondered how long she could hold him. The life jacket was practically useless; being designed for one person, it was worthless when applied to the weight of two.

She saw the endless horizon stretched out before them, the countless hours of daylight still left, and wondered if she would make it much longer. She fretted for not only the life of her husband, but also that of the unborn child she suspected was growing in her womb. Would he, or she, ever see the light of day? Just then Buck broke free from the group and swam listlessly toward them.

She realized instinctively that his pace was not from weariness or exhaustion, but instead two-fold; not only did he want to conserve his energy for the long ordeal ahead, but he didn't want to disrupt the tight-knit circle of survivors by splashing about.

Already tanned, she noticed his face was a darker shade of brown. The brim of his hat was wet and crusty with salt spray, and the ringlets of his gold curls were damp at the edges and dry and brittle above his ears.

His lips were wet but cracked from exposure as he said, "Hi Mrs. Mays. How are you holding up?"

She blushed despite herself and said, "Please, it's Kate. And we're fine," she lied, "Just fine."

"How about old Hank here?" he asked, his tense smile belying his concern.

Kate opened her mouth to impart some half-believed reassurance before closing it shut. Her chin began quivering, her lips trembling, as tears threatened to spill from her sad, frightened eyes.

"I'd pat your shoulder," buck whispered conspiratorially, sensing her tidal wave of emotions and, in part, sharing them, "but I don't want to aggravate your sunburn."

Se bit her lip and nodded as Buck swam effortlessly behind her to minister to Hank. He saw immediately that, while much of the poor man's shirt had been burned off in the searing fireball, several pieces of multi-colored fabric had been fused to his skin.

For once, he was glad for the saltwater. Not only had the moisture been able to soften the material, but the saline content had a healing property, helping to control the swelling. Gingerly, ignoring the man's pained groans; Buck pulled the shirt from Hank's skin. It was a necessary evil; to leave it there would save him the pain but could very well cost him an infection. One that was possibly life threatening.

Buck called Will and Pete over to assist him and to help hold Hank up. Several of the pieces practically float free; still others cling stubbornly to the man's blistered flesh. Blood suffuses the water around them as Buck opens old wounds to create fresh ones, but at least the ordeal is over and a wave of relief passes across Hank's face.

Kate thanked him, and after several strong words of encouragement Buck, Will and Pete floated to Lacey and Lex, where they repeated the procedure. Unfortunately, Lacey was not as brave as Kate. She complained throughout the ordeal, protesting with every rip of cloth or groan of pain from the husband leaning onto her back.

"I'm sorry, Mrs. Ross," Buck said. "If I don't do this now, it could cost him later."

Lacey shocked the group when she said, perhaps without thinking, "Can't you just let him be; make him as painless as possible?"

Fortunately, Lex had lost consciousness from the pain of Buck's procedure. The young deckhand admonished Lacey before any of her friends of family could beat him to it, "That kind of talk won't get us anywhere, ma'am. There's no telling how long this man has; to give up on him now shortens his lifespan, shortens all of our lives, so I'll have no more of it!"

To his surprise, and no doubt the rest of the survivors', instead of talking back to Buck, Lacey's face collapsed into a waterfall of tears.

"I'm sorry," she cried over and over again. "I'm so sorry, I am so sorry. I should not have said that."

Buck soothed her with more kind words; realizing much like Lex before him that the poor woman was reacting blindly, speaking without thought from her overpowering fear.

He forgave her, said a silent prayer for her husband, and then swam to each couple in turn, checking on the binds that held them together and hoping that the buoyancy of their frail life jackets would hold for the duration.

Beyond him the dolphins frolicked endlessly; they came and went at will, always keeping pace, never deserting the humans that had been so impressed with their gracefulness.

Along the way they clicked their cries of encouragement, batting their heads up and down in the water and splashing gently as if not to disrupt the tenuous ring of survivors. He nodded in their direction and didn't think he was imagining it when one of them nodded back.

"Now you're seeing things Buck," he whispered to himself as he finished his circuit and swam back into position just outside the circle. "Next you'll be seeing palm trees and hula girls!"

Aside from the searing heat and hopelessness that dogged them all, the hours had come and gone without incident when, suddenly, Ginny started to wheeze with asthma.

Her husband, Pete, recognized the telltale wheezing and was immediately alarmed. Her condition was aggravated by the fact that each time she gasped for air some of the salty water that surrounded them leaked into her open mouth; she was soon choking as well as gasping.

Pete tried to remain calm; he had to, to help his wife. As the rest of the survivors watched helplessly he talked to her in a soothing voice, giving her room so that she could keep her chin above water and helping her through the attack.

It was all he could do; all he had was his wits and her good sense; they both knew that to survive the attack she would have to remain calm, try to soothe her shattered nerves and allow the oxygen to flow more freely through her constricted airway.

Slowly, but not without great pain and self-sacrifice, the attack lessened. Ginny was weak and nauseous with the intake of saltwater, and vomited several times, exacerbating her condition until, at last, her breathing became better, but still irregular and Pete could once again cling to her still trembling back.

The eyes of her concerned friends and family remained glued to the young couple, Ginny in particular, until all were assured that the worst had passed. Her wheezing continued, but thankfully the choking and panic as a thing of the past.

At least for now…

Soon new ills took precedence over the old: they all became victims of needle fish and silver dollar sized crabs. From out of nowhere they came, floating adrift the ocean currents and affixing themselves to the struggling survivors with surprisingly firm grips.

The crabs, especially, proved torturous as their tiny pincers tortured them below the water level as surely as the sun did above it. At first the women squealed, surprised by the sudden onslaught of crusty hitchhikers but when they realized the offenders were hear to stay, they soon got busy pulling them away with fingers that quickly grew bloody and tender. They tried kicking them off, pulling them, punching them, batting them away, but like the sun they seemed to return two-fold. It became an ongoing ordeal, an endless battle between human and crab.

Meanwhile the smaller needlefish proved just as worthy a foe. Little sucking lips and teeth wriggled between folds of the women's blouses or the men's shorts and attacked any exposed skin.

They needled into nooks and crannies the crabs could not go, so that the suffering proved twice as torturous. Like a ripple effect the tight-knit circle shook, and rolled with the effort of keeping the bloodsuckers at bay. Had their situation not been so critical, the pain not so intense, the vision might have actually been humorous.

It was worse still for the two burned men, Lex and Hank, who in addition to the usual suspects of crabs and needlefish soon attracted the larger, hungrier mouths of small but no less ravenous fish, who fed off their still bleeding wounds and caused intense pain with each and every tiny nibble.

Silently, the group wondered if it could get any worse.

To a one, they all seemed to know it most certainly could…

None in the water realized the dolphins were swimming in and around the group—keeping predators away.

Quietly, underwater, swiftly moving over and over the dolphins butted sharks in the side if they came too near. They were on guard…

CHAPTER 11

Setting Sun; Bolstered Spirits

Buck watched anxiously as the sun began its downward arc over the horizon. The water lapped gently against the group, still clinging to each other as they had been all day, the lazy breeze yawning in from the west at last cooling their sunburned skin with its soft kisses of genuine, if brief, relief.

It was a welcome respite from the grueling day they'd spent suffering under the blistering and relentless sun. It had been silent for the last few hours, each survivor dealing in his or her own way with their immense grief.

Then, too, Buck knew they were simply awed into silence by the sheer tragedy they faced. His frequent assurances, not to mention desperate prayers, that a search party would find them had gone unheeded, and by the late hour he knew that the time when they were scheduled to return to Yankeetown had finally come and gone.

Their berth would be empty, their slip unfilled even as the rest of the boats, bit and small, found their way home to Yankeetown in the waning afternoon light. Still, even that offered little hope. Had it been a weekday, perhaps, someone on the bustling if modest pier might have noticed the absence.

A fellow captain and first mate lingering over a cold beer at the bait shack might have commented to each other about Hazy Days absence, deciding to open another and wait until it arrived, perhaps even offer a helping hand if the catch was unusually large.

But today was Sunday; captains, mates, and passengers alike would be eager to dock, feel dry land beneath their feet, and head home before the sun set and enjoy what remained of their precious Sunday evening.

There would be no lingering over cold beer at the already closed bait shack, no observant eyes noticing the boat' empty slip. There would be only people in a hurry, and neither the empty slip nor the passengers' cars still parked in the grassy lot nearby would mean anything to those heading home.

Late arrivals back to Yankeetown were just as common as early ones, and a Skipper's clock worked on one time and one time only, and that was fish time. Bait and hooks were their hour and minute hands, and it was often the passengers, not the crew, who questioned, "Isn't it time to be heading home now?"

Sunday or no, few captains would begrudge their passengers an extra hour on the sea if the grouper were hitting fast and furious, and there were just as many Sundays Buck could remember docking two hours late as arriving two hours early.

Buck's stomach churned with worry and doubt. Perhaps he alone fully understood the enormity of their situation. It was a weight he would have preferred to share, but t the same time a burden he wouldn't wish on anyone. Ignorance, in this case, truly *was* bliss. Though the other men aboard may have been older and wiser, Buck was a man of the sea and knew the desperate hours that awaited them.

Night would come, and with it the fear of the unknown—not to mention the *unseen*. Daylight was bad enough; when one could see the crabs and needlefish that plagued them all. But as darkness fell each tiny nibble, each fin against skin would magnify in size until it would seem as if the entire ocean would be feasting on their burnt skin.

Buck cleared his throat, noticing the way his dry, chapped lips had trouble parting, and said without a hint of doubt in his voice, "I'm afraid it may be a few more hours until our rescue arrives. It suddenly occurred to me that I don't know very much about, well, *any* of you. Do you mind if each of you tells us a little something about yourself? It may seem silly at this point but, I think you'll all agree that there are less pleasant ways to pass the time."

"You mean like floating in silence?" quipped Bill, ever the jokester.

Nervous laughter greeted his remark; until at last Kate began by saying "My husband and I are going to have a baby, in about five or five and a half months." Despite the enormity of this revelation, her husband, Hank, was in too much pain to respond. Kate was trying to stay positive.

As the news rippled from person to person Buck silenced the whispers by offering a hearty "congratulations." Sensing the awkwardness in which the news had been greeted, he decided to ask, "Do you have a preference, Kate? I mean, do you want a boy or a girl?"

Hank, silent and unavailable in his pain, merely bobbed along as Kate smiled nervously and admitted, "Well, I would love to have a little girl, but Hank where wouldn't mind a junior, I know. It's always been his dream to stop selling cars and run his own dealership, so perhaps 'little Hank' wouldn't mind working at 'Hank & Sons Motors.' Isn't that right, honey?"

Though Kate had posed the question, the forced smile on her face told Buck she expected no answer in return. In silence, the group nodded politely though Buck knew they all saw what he saw: a desperate, pained, ravaged man barely clinging to life and in no position to drive a car let alone sell one.

Would Hank survive the ordeal?

Buck had no idea.

It depended on a variety of variables, he supposed, not the least of which involved the man's inner strength and constitution. Was he a fighter? Or a quitter? Only time, Buck knew, would tell. His burns were severe, and required immediate attention from a trained physician.

That much, at least, was certain…

Floating listlessly in lukewarm saltwater while the sun beat down on you did not bode well for his or, for that matter, *any* of their survival. What the man needed was a soft bed, clean bandages, a team of nurses and a qualified doctor to begin treating his wounds immediately.

Then again, Buck had heard tales around the docks of men who'd survived worse and come through it alive; many of them skippered or worked aboard boats until they retired happily to sit around the very same docks and tell tall tales of their heroic survival until their final days.

Still, Buck had his doubts. This was a hearty group, no doubt. They were young, fit, happy, and seemed to be resilient enough to weather most storms. The women, in particular, glowed with an inner strength that defied all logic.

Here they were, lugging their husbands on their sun-blistered backs and dog-paddling the day away, and still congratulating each other on birth announcements. Would wonders never cease?

And yet Buck knew everyone had their own breaking point. For some it would be hunger, for others it would be thirst. Still others would buckle under the heat, or the crabs, or the fish, or a combination of all of the above.

So far they'd endured much, and all but one had survived. And yet the afternoon was far from over. More challenges awaited them. Each hour without water sapped them of their strength and drained them of their energy. Each hour spent kicking their legs meant cramps and backaches and sore muscles and complaints. The worst, he feared, was far from over.

How many, Buck wondered, *would last the night?*

"That sounds like a mighty fine plan," Buck replied at last, breaking the awkward silence that had followed Kate's startling revelation. "I know no matter what you have, a little Kate to hang on your apron strings of a Hank Jr., it will come as a comfort to you after we are all home safe. Anyone else?"

Sunny smiled hesitantly, tempted to raise her hand as if she were in Sunday school but deciding at the last minute to simply blurt out the fact that her mom and sisters, Anne and Wanda, were watching over their three kid.

"I can just picture them now," she said, eyes looking over the heads of her companions, "running my poor mother ragged and putting their aunts to the test. I can't wait to hear the reports, good and bad, when we get home."

Her husband, Will, as if to mollify his own concerns, added weakly, "Our daughter is extremely capable also, so we are not in the least concerned about how our kids are faring. We know they are in good hands."

The group nodded, their chins making lapping sounds in the water as they bobbed up and down, the longest of the women's hair floating like seaweed out behind them.

Buck was suddenly struck by the incongruity of their situation; here they were, floating in the middle of the ocean, carrying on a conversation as if they were at an ice cream social instead of stranded miles out to sea.

He couldn't help but smile…

Instantly, the effort made his chapped lips cry out in protest as he licked them, dryly, once more. Out of nowhere Pete said, "Ginny and I would love to have a child of our own soon. Right, honey?"

Ginny was still wheezing but managed to respond, "Yes, when this is over, we want to start a family right away."

Buck watched as the two gave each other a reassuring smile. They looked so young and handsome; he could easily imagine a brood of similarly pretty children running around their house.

Throughout the trip he'd been impressed by their obvious affection for each other. Once or twice he'd heard the term "love birds" tossed about by their fellow passengers—some times happily, other times enviously—and he smiled to think how apt a term it was in describing them.

He couldn't help but wonder how he and his own wife, Betty Jo, would manage in such a disaster, but he hoped it would be just as these two did: with loving tenderness and unconditional support for each other, in good time and in bad.

As Ginny had struggled for breath earlier in the afternoon he'd watched as Pete whispered to her soothingly, his words like a balm to the frightened woman as she fought against her own body to bring breath into her lungs. How courageous the two seemed; how courageous they *all* seemed.

Lacey, thoroughly frightened and exhausted by now, blurted out as if someone had challenged her, "Lex and I have three wonderful children, and I just wish I could go home right now to be with them, they'll be worried. I told them we would be home before bed time."

The other women nodded feverishly, as if praying, and Buck heard several of the men murmur in kind. Thought the group seemed to have a strained relationship with the feisty woman, her ways were easily forgiven as she voiced the opinions of the entire group: "I just wish I could go home…"

Didn't they all?

Bill Saunders spoke for both he and his wife, saying, "Lois's Mom is at our house with our three children, so we don't have to worry one bit about them."

Again, Buck was reminded of the importance of family to this tight-knit group. Through complaints and fear had been their initial reaction to their involuntary plunge into the sea, and later when the sun had begun to beat down on them and the fish and crustaceans to feast, now they seemed more resilient, more resigned, more concerned with the family and friends back home than their own safety.

Again and again Buck heard it in their voices: "…our kids are safe, that's all that matter."

Even if they didn't say it like that, exactly, he knew that's what they meant. Knew it the same way he knew the dark was but minutes away; and with It the new fear of survival through that night.

Lois shyly smiled at these encouraging words, and asked everyone to stop and pray "The Lord's Prayer."

With the gentle sound of lapping water providing a choral hymn for the background music, one by one their voices lifted into prayer as they whispered in unison:

> *Our Father,*
> *Who art in heaven,*
> *Hallow'd be Thy Name.*
> *Thy kingdom come,*
> *Thy will be done*

On earth as it is in heaven.
Give us this day our daily bread,
And forgive us our debts,
As we forgive our debtors.
And lead us not into temptation,
But deliver us from evil,
For Thine is the kingdom
And the power,
And the glory,
Forever.
Amen...

Even after the words were spoken, silence remained as quiet, unspoken prayers were offered in the wake of "Amen." After the prayer, spirits seemed lifted, their fears diminished, smiles temporarily affixed to silently moving lips. Buck noticed a smile or two among the group, even as the day's dwindling sunlight dappled off the water and caught in their eyes.

The youngest survivors, Sam and Analee, winked conspiratorially at each other and finally managed to tell everyone that they had just been "pinned" and were hoping for a bright future together. Their excitement was infectious; their attraction to each other obvious, their youth enviable.

Analee's sunburned skin glowed a fiery red but her eyes glowed even brighter as she said, "We've been so busy worrying about the tiny details; Sam's degree, my work, the distance between us. Now it seems all that matters is each other."

Again, heads nodded vigorously in agreement.

"You're so right, Analee," echoed Kate. "For so long Hank and I have gone back and forth about having a child and whether or not we could afford it; now those problems seem so minor."

Another chorus of nods greeted the comment as, perhaps giving thanks; the group once again fell into an almost reverent silence. Buck smiled to himself; he'd accomplished his goal of taking everyone's mind off their current troubles, including his own!

Almost as an afterthought, Bill Saunders asked Buck about his family. With a smile, the young sailor described his lovely wife, Betty Jo, and their three spunky children. His eyes shone pride, "They run their momma ragged but she loves it. They look just like her, and love the outdoors like me."

Buck's voice had grown hoarse, and he noticed the others seemed to be wilting as well. The afternoon heat continued to plague them, though at least it had gone down from a raging boil as at midday to a slow, steady simmer as the light slowly dimmed.

Around them the lapping waves gave little relief; thirst ravaged their bodies and each time the salt water threatened to lap at their dry, chapped lips it was so tempting to simply take a swallow relieve their unquenched thirst.

But Buck had warned them thoroughly, almost vehemently, against it. "Trust me," he had said, his eyes grim and dark with the implied warning, "the quick relief will fade and you'll be worse off."

He was referring, of course to the physical ills that could result from swallowing saltwater. Not the least of which included nausea, vomiting, dehydration, and a possibly lethal imbalance in the body's water-filled cells from a sudden infusion of salt into one's delicate system.

Perhaps worst of all, Buck knew, was a raging desire to repeat the cycle, over and over again, ingesting more saltwater to quench more of the thirst the salt itself produced. It was a never ending and heartbreaking cycle. Buck was glad he had never witnessed it firsthand.

Nor was he eager to do so now...

Buck eyed the horizon and noticed the sun would soon set. He knew they would need their energy for the next 12 hours—it was unlikely that, even if someone noticed them missing, a search party would commence before dawn.

Idly he wondered how long his own family would wait before alerting the authorities. Sadly, Betty Jo was all too used to Buck coming home late from a long day of fishing, be it Sunday or Tuesday, and her busy schedule of taking care of three kids often found her falling asleep long before he returned home.

He cleared his throat once more and, after he had the group's full attention, went on to say, "We should rest now and pray that God is sending help our way very soon. Let's check our ties to each other before we try to rest.

The group agreed silently, nodding their heads, as most too Buck's words as gospel. Not all, though. As night finally fell on Sunday, only the voices of Ginny and Sunny were loud enough for all to hear.

Sunny said, her voice barely above a whisper, "Remember our big sister deal. I've always looked after you because you're my baby sister and I'm not going to stop now. Just hang on."

Ginny, who was still coughing and wheezing, merely nodded her head. She wanted so badly to believe Sunny, but she was so tired, so thirsty, no matter what Sunny said or did.

Her last attack had scared her so badly; she didn't think she'd pull through. The moments had been torturous; her labored breathing only an outward sign of her inner turmoil.

How long would she last before another attack struck? What if Pete couldn't talk her through the next one? Was it fair to drag him down with her weakness? Would be better off without her?

The dark thoughts clouded her mind even as the dark sky appeared, too soon, blanketing them all in an uneasy sea of dread and unease. As Ginny battled her own demons, the rest of the survivors followed suit.

Though darkness had fallen and sleep threatened to overtake them, a more immediate fear threatened to keep them all on their toes: Everyone was constantly pulling the attached crabs off their water-logged life jackets—and themselves.

It became a litany throughout the early evening; the tugging of claws and the splashing o the crusty offenders being thrown back into the deep. Winces of pain battled with cries of frustration as one by one, the passengers fought off the determined little creatures.

Just as Buck suspected, the darkness only made their suffering worse. Though tiny, the crabs grew exponentially with each passing hour until at last they seemed to be gargantuan creatures clinging to their backs, their thighs, their feet, their hair.

Sunny struggled to keep her composure as several times her fellow female passengers leaked silent tears into the cooling sea. There was little to do but join them, and amazingly, they all felt better after a good cry. If only Will would break down his tough exterior and follow suit.

Little did she know that not all the water dripping onto her shoulders came from the sea…

CHAPTER 12

Missing

Lynn Morgan, Analee's by now very worried mother, stared at the clock on her kitchen wall for the sixth time in as many minutes. She didn't like what she saw. Nor could she believe it.

"Where in the world," she asked aloud, no longer worried about what the neighbors might think of a crazy woman who talked to herself, "could Analee be?" she was alone at the kitchen table, an uneaten plate of dinner sitting before her.

Across from her, Analee's place setting was poignantly empty as well. Lynn had been expecting to fry up some fresh grouper for dinner, she'd even fried up some hush puppies and made tartar sauce from scratch using her own mother's closely guarded recipe, but the evening meal had come and gone and, along with it, her appetite.

For over three hours she had paced an uneven tread in the kitchen floor, until at last she had simply heated up some soup and made herself a sandwich of cold cuts and fresh cheese, stowing the hush puppies and tartar sauce in the icebox for Analee's eventual homecoming. Now it lay uneaten before her, the soup long cold, the bread crust long since dried out.

She pushed it away with a clicking of her tongue and sighed. Her daughter should be home. She had work tomorrow, she hadn't called, and it was unlike Analee not to at least call.

Lynn had waited long enough. She'd gone through all the scenarios in her head, trying to keep herself from making a foolish mistake and getting all worked up over something that might just as well have been easily explained away as a fit of schoolgirl whimsy.

But Analee was no longer in school and, even when she had been, this kind of oversight would have been out of character for the responsible Analee. True, Analee was a fun loving girl, but she would have called…

Perhaps Analee and Sam had decided to have dinner after their long day at sea, she has thought at first. But that hadn't seemed quite right, either. She would have been ready for a shower and her job was too important to her to jeopardize for something as silly as an extra slice of pie at the late-night diner on Sunday night. Even Sam had better sense that that; as important as Analee's job was to her his schooling was to Sam.

Then she'd thought that perhaps Analee and Sam had gotten a flat tire on the way home. Sam's car—Analee jokingly referred to it as "That old jalopy"—wasn't the most reliable of transportation. He wasn't a mechanic but something as simple as a dead battery or flat tire would be no problem for the young man. Perhaps he might have lost half an hour to the minor malfunction, but nearly three? Never.

Perhaps the boat had been delayed by bad weather at sea. But Lynn had been listening to the radio all day for signs of bad weather and heard none, let alone seen any. A quick check outside her door had revealed clear skies and little cloud cover. How different could the weather be thirty miles away?

No, something, she knew, had happened…

Never before had 8:30 p.m. felt so cold, dark, and desolate.

A slight chill came over Lynn as she stared at the clock once more. She had promised to give herself three hours before panicking and contacting authorities, as if that magic number would somehow find Analee walking up the front porch in her new sandals smelling of fresh fish and salt spray.

But what did it matter anymore? Two hours or three? One hour or four? No matter how Lynn Morgan looked at it, the boat and its passengers were, by now, long overdue.

Wringing her hands, Lynn finally placed a call to the Florida Highway Patrol.

"H-h-hello," she stammered to the pleasant-sounding operator who announced herself, "this is Lynn Morgan."

"My daughter and a group of friends left this morning on a one-day grouper fishing trip. They should have returned well before this. Has an accident been reported—they would be coming from the Yankeetown Dock."

Sergeant Robert Thomas of the Highway Patrol answered the call. "No, ma'am," he said after being transferred from the main switchboard and apprised of the particulars of the situation, "there have been no accidents reported at this time. Maybe they just got a late start back. Why don't you let me do some further checking, and I'll call you back?"

"Oh thanks so much," Lynn said, relieved at last to share her news with someone else. Almost as an afterthought she hurriedly added, "My number is MA7294."

Sergeant Thomas was a family man. Getting off the phone with Lynn Morgan, and hearing the emotion in her voice; Sergeant Thomas knew his wife would have sounded the same way if something was wrong with one of their kids. He decided to personally look into Analee's disappearance.

Getting inside his three-year-old police cruiser, Sergeant Thomas drove off into the night. There was no need for lights or sirens at this point, not yet anyway, but his pace was brisk nonetheless. He'd brought coffee in his thermos, but had no idea whether he'd need one cup, or the whole canteen.

Unlike some areas of Florida, Tampa, perhaps, or the state capitol in Tallahassee, Ocala was no booming metropolis. By 8:30 in the evening, particularly on the Sabbath, one could almost see where the town had rolled up its sidewalks and put them away for the night.

Only the late night diner had its lights blazing, but even that was on account of the policemen and firefighters who would be changing shifts in a few hours. After that, there was nothing doing in the small, close-knit community until early Monday morning when the milk bottles began rattling in old Joe's delivery truck or the *Ocala Star-Banner* slammed against porch screens, announcing a brand new day.

Sergeant Thomas cruised through the empty streets, checking nearby roads for a stalled car as his headlights pierced the inky dark, he got on his radio speaking with Sheriff's Deputy Matt McGuire and inquiring as to what his next step might be.

He knew what he should do, of course, but chain of command required he go by the book. This could be a simple traffic problem, or it could be something much more serious. After several minutes the two men decided to check the parking area at the Yankeetown dock, where the couple would have left their car.

Sergeant Thomas hung up the radio and drove his car, sipping from his second cup of lukewarm coffee as the speedometer cruised steadily at 50 miles per hour. There was a faint unease niggling at his sour stomach, and it had little to do with the notoriously bad brew from the precinct's ancient coffee urn.

Yankeetown was closed up tight by the time he met up with Chief Deputy McGuire, their cruisers idling in the parking lot as Sergeant Thomas checked license plates until he found the car belonging to Analee's boyfriend.

The two men nodded grimly at each other, wiping sweat from their brows and peering at the deserted docks as if they might yield the solutions to all their troubles. It was clear the passengers had made the boat, and since the berth belonging to the Hazy Days was still empty, that something had happened while they were at sea.

"Sergeant Thomas," McGuire sighed as he stared down the row of idle cars just to their left. "We've got a problem here. You've got a boat out there with a dozen passengers, and crew, and they're now officially four hours overdue. Something tells me that boat ran into trouble."

Sergeant Thomas nodded, but countered, explaining, "I know the captain and crew of the Hazy Days, sir. They're good men. Why, Buck's reliable and Captain Wilson's been fishing these waters as long as I've been playing cops and robbers. If something's happened, I dare say those two men could handle just about anything."

McGuire frowned, stating "Thomas, I need to call in Sheriff Harris." For he too knew the crew and he knew he was right. Everything from engine failure to rough seas, to rogue waves to, well, mutiny—stranger things had happened out there or so the fisherman said at the local barber shop—that could trip up a captain and his crew, no matter how experienced they might be.

McGuire lent an ear to the silent night; only the chirpings of a forest full of crickets answered him. "Well," he sighed, "there's nothing we can do here tonight. Call one of your uniformed officers and have him park himself here for the night. On the off chance that the Hazy Days limps into port, we'll want someone with a radio car to alert us immediately."

"You really think they'll be able to come in on their own steam?" Sergeant Thomas asked. McGuire merely shook his head. "you head back to headquarters and get Mrs. Morgan on the phone; tell her what we've found and ask her to start a round robin with the other family members. I don't want you tying up the phone lines repeating what little we have to say to six different families in six different ways. After that, all we can do is wait."

"Why is that?" asked Sergeant Thomas, recalling the stricken sound of Mrs. Morgan's voice.

"Can't send a search party out until morning, Thomas."

The words "Search party" sent a chill up the young sergeant's spine. The two men made quick chit-chat before getting back in their respective cars and driving off in opposite directions into the night.

Back at the precinct, Deputy McGuire made quick work of assigning a rookie to wait at the Yankeetown lot. "Wait," he said, hanging the eager but untested greenhorn his half-empty thermos jug. "Swing by the break room on your way out there and grab some fresh coffee for yourself. Make sure it's strong and black. Chances are you'll need it. I'll be by in the morning to relieve you."

The fresh-scrubbed young man took off with a quick salute and a wave of the shiny silver thermos over his shoulder. McGuire couldn't help but hide a smile; he wouldn't be so enthusiastic six hours from now staring at the same six license plates all night.

"Ah, the joys of youth," he sighed aloud as he dialed the number for Sheriff John Harris, "Boss, you need to come down here, we have a problem."

Sheriff Harris answered and drove straight to his office. John Harris immediately took over and telephoned Mrs. Morgan himself.

"Yes," her rapid breathing made it sound as if she'd just come in from running a marathon. "Have you found them yet? Are they all right? Where can I pick them up? They must be starving by n—"

"No," Harris interrupted a tad too brusquely, He regretted it immediately, but the fact remained that he was none too eager to get the woman's hopes up further than they already were.

"I'm sorry, Ma'am," he continued, "but when we got out there to Yankeetown we discovered the young man's car. In fact, all the cars of the boat's passengers were accounted for, as well as the captain's truck. I've conferred with my officers, Ma'am, and they inform me that the boat may have run into some engine troubles.

"Please don't be alarmed; we're sure everything is fine and that by sunup the boat and its passengers will limp into port under its own power. If not, we're prepared to alert the Coast Guard and launch a full out search for your daughter and her—"

"The Coast Guard!?!" shrieked Lynn Morgan, practically dropping the phone. "Is it *that* serious?"

Sheriff Harris tried his best to reassure the panicked mother, but he feared his half-hearted attempt at putting a positive spin on the situation only made things worse.

"Please, Mrs. Morgan, I know it sounds serious, but this is what the Coast Guard does. 99% of their job, in fact, is to rescue stranded boaters. They call it 'job security.' It's a very routine matter in this day and age; nothing to be worried about at all. I'm sure come daybreak, if your daughter's not home by then, the Coast Guard will be able to retrieve her and the rest of the passengers by lunchtime."

"What can I do until then, Sheriff Harris?" He replied, "Call the other families please. I'm afraid all any of us can do is wait, Ma'am. And, of course, pray."

"Amen to that," said the fearful mother without a trace of irony. The two exchanged several pleasantries before hanging up, but for Lynn, the night was just beginning.

First she called the other family members, as Sheriff Harris had urged her to do. (As if she'd need the reminder!) Although it was far from a pleasant task, she was relieved to see that once she'd called the final family members and told them the news, several more hours had passed.

She feared none of them would find sleep this night...

At last she traded in her stale dinner and cold soup to start a fresh pot of coffee, filling the house with light as she waited for it to brew. She lit a candle at the kitchen table and watched it burn down, hour after hour.

She paced from room to room, laying out her clothes for the next morning and writing herself little notes and leaving them where she could see: "Call Analee's work in the morning."

By midnight, her kitchen table was cluttered with little scraps of paper. They were clearly visible in the flickering candlelight as she passed by during another marathon session of pacing.

She simply couldn't help it. "Where is Analee?" she asked herself again and again. "Where is my daughter?"

From time to time she stilled her pacing, standing in front of an open window and staring out into the night. Her reflection was clearly visible in the thick, lead-paned glass thanks to all the lights behind her, but still she cupped her chin in her hand and seemed to stare beyond her reflection.

Beyond lay the dark night. Even on dry land the nearly black outside seemed endless; Lynn could only imagine what it might have looked like thirty miles out to sea!

Poor Analee; she was so brave but how frightened she must be now, but if anyone could stay positive it was her, she could just imagine her turning this mishap into an adventure.

She could hardly wait to hear the story Analee would tell about this trip. She herself was trying to think positive; they were just late in returning, nothing more, after all, the weather was so calm…

Lynn sighed, her breath falling heavy on the thick-paned glass. She turned, unsteady on her feet, to gaze at the clock once more. A gasp escaped her constricted throat; she was shocked to see nearly an hour had passed since she'd stopped at the window.

Why, it had felt like only minutes…

And so the evening passed; Lynn paced, and stopped, and stared, and paced, and stared, and stopped. One pot of coffee came and went, another was sputtering soundly as the dark of night at last gave way to the purple of dawn.

Still she realized it was too soon to call Sheriff Harris, who must surely have had other cases he was working on. And so another hour passed, then another, the black draining to purple, the purple giving way to pink, the pink fading to a brilliant blue, as at long last, Monday morning dawned bright and early.

Only then would Lynn allow herself to dial the direct number Sheriff Harris had given her. Even though he answered on the second ring, his voice sounded strained as the two began an awkward conversation.

"I wish I had better news, Mrs. Morgan," he started, struggling to stifle a yawn. Around him the station house was likewise yawning to life as a shift change swelled the halls with those officers thick and bleary-eyed from ending a shift and others wide-eyed at beginning a new one.

He cringed, realizing it was the wrong way to start with a mother who, no doubt, had been pacing her house since they last spoke.

"Why?" she asked, confirming her fears. "Has something happened?"

"No, no ma'am. I merely meant that my man at the docks reports there's been no new activity. Officially, the Hazy Days has been listed as missing. We've yet to explain why but I have to be honest, if the motor has broken down, they might need some help getting back to port. I'll make some calls, get a search started, and see what needs to be done. At this point, I'm afraid; it's the best I can do. I'm sorry, Mrs. Morgan."

Lynn nodded, forgetting Sheriff Harris couldn't see her.

"Mrs. Morgan?" he asked pointedly, none too eager for her to lose her focus at this stage of the game. "Ma'am? Are you there?"

"Sorry, Sheriff Harris," she replied at last. "Yes, yes I'm here, just trying to take this all in. You hear about these things, you know, but you never imagine it could really happen to you."

"Don't jump the gun, Ma'am. We're not sure anything has happened yet. I don't want you to be overconfident and, at the same time, I don't want you borrowing trouble. It could be something as minor as an empty tank of gas."

"Do you really believe that, sir?"

"Ma'am," he said, more honestly this time, "I really don't know what to believe at this point. I'm as much in the dark as you are right now. I can promise you this, though: you stay by the phone and I promise to keep you posted as soon as I have any news. I'm sorry, ma'am, but it's simply the best I can do. Can you do me a favor and do another round robin? Let the other families know what I've just told you?"

Harris was relieved when Lynn Morgan agreed to be his diplomat with the families of those aboard the Hazy Days. With that task off his plate and onto hers, he decided to notify the Coast Guard for assistance.

Even with the cavalry on its way, Harris felt restless as he hung up the phone. If the ship had broken down, as he suspected, it would be useless for transporting its passengers.

With the Coast Guard vessel otherwise occupied in seeing to the distressed craft, additional boats would be needed to transfer the captain, his crew, and the passengers back to Yankeetown and, he assumed, the nearest hospital for observation and, after a day and night of exposure, possible treatment for sunburn and/or dehydration.

He grabbed his spare thermos, filled it up, and headed down to Yankeetown by now the dock would be buzzing about the empty berth normally reserved for the Hazy Days, and he would need to recruit several boat captains before they set off on their appointed rounds.

He made a mental list as he drove, the sound of his siren alerting other drivers of his need for speed. The trip, he knew, was only scheduled for one day. That meant limited supplies to start with, and definitely not enough for more than one day in case of emergency.

There was no telling how far the boat could have drifted without power, or how far it had gone before the first signs of trouble. It might take all afternoon to locate the boat, if not longer, and after one day and one night at sea, those on board would not only be victims of the elements but hungry and thirsty as well.

On the back of a blank speeding citation, he made a list as he drove. He knew he'd promised to relieve that greenhorn as soon as daybreak, but instead he would send him for supplies.

The rescue boats should carry extra food and water.

CHAPTER 13

Breakfast, Anyone?

The sun dawned early for the survivors, cresting just after six. There was no land in sight, no boats either, for that matter, only the sunburned and withered faces of the family and friends now in the water for nearly 24-hours now.

Eyes swollen, mouths dry and cracked, it took a few moments for the group to stir and wake up. Heads were groggy; lips stuck together, noses running from the constant bombardment of rich, musky salt air that had assailed them throughout the night.

As they stirred the critters that had attached themselves like barnacles to their shoulders, necks, and hair skittered about; a dozen or more splashes could be heard as shivers and panic sent them back into the sea.

It was quite a wake-up call for the groggy crowd...

The women couldn't help but grown in protest as their husbands struggled for purchase upon their backs, but one woman realized with a start that her husband was no longer there: Kate Mays.

She gasped in shock to feel the sudden weightlessness on her sunburned shoulders, turning in circles to see if perhaps he'd merely readjusted himself to give her a chance to rest her aching muscles and ease out the cramp that had been plaguing her throughout the night.

Her discovery was like a ripple cast out through the ocean; slowly the rest of the group realized that Hank Mays was no longer clinging to his wife's back, and had gradually slipped away and disappeared into the water during the night.

Kate panicked, screaming hysterically as the rest of the group watched her helplessly. She wailed into the endless blue sky, splashed her hands in the water, alerting the dolphins who were hovering nearby that something was amiss. Suddenly, all the women were shaken up. Some of them started to sob, others tried to comfort her—all of them talking at once as Kate's shrieks turned to sobs turned to whimpers turned to silence.

Buck closed his eyes, said a silent prayer, and turned to the man nearest him, whispering almost plaintively, "Help me?"

Bill nodded grimly, but dutifully, and said, "Of course." Together the two separated from the group and swam in opposite directions of each other, figuring they could cover more ground that way before meeting up again where they'd started.

Buck swam slowly, kicking with his feet, aware that only if Hank had somehow managed to slip off his wife's back in the last few minutes would such a surface search actually find him. His efforts stirred up the needlefish and crabs that constantly clung to his deck short and shoulders, but little else.

Bill found much the same; he moved slowly, averting the eyes of the other men and listening as the women tried in vain to comfort one of their own. He couldn't help but think of his own mortality as he faced this grim task.

The sea seemed endless. What use was it to search a few dozen square feet when around them lapped hundreds of endless nautical miles. He shuddered, picturing Hank having to give up the fight and simply drifting down into the ocean's endless depths.

Had he been fearful? Or blissfully peaceful, thinking only of stopping the agonizing pain that must have riddled his body as the burns began festering and continued throughout the long, brutal day they'd shared together as friends.

Their last, apparently...

For once he was glad to be surrounded by so much water. "Goodbye, old friend," he murmured to himself as he pictured Hank's scarred, sunburned body drifting downward. How dark it must have seemed, how heavy and sad and endless.

"Rest in peace," he murmured as he heard the familiar sound of Buck splashing quietly nearby. As the two men looked at each other, he saw in Buck's eyes the same fear and helplessness he himself felt.

Buck quietly shook his head and Bill returned the gesture. Hank was gone, Bill knew, and no amount of searching was going to bring him back. What would Kate do now?

For that matter, what would any of them do?

Bill looked at Buck as he hovered around Kate, struggling, Bill knew, for the right words to say. It was the first time, Bill realized, he had thought of the responsibility for their safety that this young man must feel.

Buck had taken the loss of the captain calmly, stoically, taking great pains to move forward and never look back. But now it was as if the grief snuck up on him, smacking him all at once. Even though Kate was too absorbed by her own tidal wave of pain to realize it, Bill watched proudly as Buck placed a gentle hand on her shoulder to calm her.

It mattered little. Kate was still hysterical; no matter what the other women did she simply could not be consoled. Finally, Analee said to her, "Please, Kate, you have to stop crying. This can't be good for you or the baby. You have to hang on for the baby's sake and your own."

She paused, looking to the other women for support. One by one, they nodded knowingly; glad that someone had finally said what had been on all of their minds. They urged the youngest of them on with kind eyes and simple nods, their long hair making quiet splashing noises in the water.

Thus emboldened, Analee continued: "We're here for you, Kate, all of us, and *will* help you get through this. Keep your head up and be careful not to swallow any of the seawater. Think of getting home and being with your baby. Isn't that what Hank would have wanted?"

At her husband's name, Kate's sobs quietly subsided, but the vacant look in her eyes remained. Her hopelessness was palpable to one and all; it spread through the water like blood, reaching them all, covering them all in its sorrow and pain and threatening to suck them all down with it.

First the Captain.

Now Hank.

Who would be next?

Buck swam over to Bill and explained, "Look, you know all of the passengers. Let's keep them talking. It will keep their spirits up. But don't let them swallow any salt water."

He saw Bill's panicked expression and quickly added an explanation, "It's almost been 24 hours, everyone's thirsty and it will be tempting, but it'll be deadly. Keep their minds off of it. I'll watch over Mrs. Mays while you are doing that."

Bill nodded, watching Buck drift slowly toward the grieving widow.

His admiration for the brave young man grew by degrees…

Bill cleared his dry, parched throat and said, "All right everyone, you missed breakfast. Tell me what you want to eat and I'll take your order. Honey, I'll start with you."

Lois realized it might be nice to think of something other than death and their grim fate for a change. She thought for only a second before admitting, "Oh, I'd just like some oatmeal and coffee, dear. That's all for me."

Bill "waited on" Will next.

Will replied solemnly, looking as uncomfortable as if he'd just walked into the ladies room instead of the men's, "I don't feel like playing, Bill, but I know what you're trying to do, so I will anyway. Give me an omelet. Sunny, you know the kind I like, all gooey with cheese, mushrooms, and ham."

Sunny grinned, getting into the act and adding, "I surely do know, honey, and I'll take the same, Bill, but add some fried potatoes with that, please. I don't know about you, but I'm extra hungry this morning."

Bill nodded, lifting his waterlogged hands from the sea and pretending to write out Sunny and Will's order on a pad. He gave them a quick thumbs-up sign before nodding in Pete's direction. "Your turn, you two lovebirds."

Pete smiled weakly, then turned to his wife. He added quietly, "Ginny, what would you like? Anything you want. It's on me!"

Ginny was having trouble breathing and, despite the sunburn shared by them all, looked pale and grim as day break. Even so, she rasped out her ordering labored breaths, never one to dampen another's mood if she could help it: "I'd like some toast with Mama's guava jelly spread all over it, please."

The comforting thought made her smile...

Lex was unable to speak because of his burns and constant pain, so Lacey spoke for both of them when she orderd, "Hot tea, please, with plenty of lemon and sugar. For both of us please."

Bill smiled, thinking to himself how wise Buck had been to suggest this. Keeping in the spirit of the game, he acted like the first page of his pad was flipped and mimed turning another before gazing at the youngest couple in the group.

"Analee?" he asked quietly. "Sam?"

Analee looked at Sam before turning back to Bill. "We would rather have two big, juicy cheeseburgers, home fries, and two large cherry Cokes," she said, gazing wistfully into the water as if remembering every detail of that innocent, carefree night, "just like the ones we had Saturday night."

For his part, poor Sam could not speak. He had nothing left in him, not even spit, with which to place his own order. His lips were parched and cracked. He could only nod and try to give a halfway smile.

Gone was the vibrant boy who'd come to pick Analee up at her mother's house only a day—had it just been a day?!?—before. In his place was a shell of a man; his eyes drained of life, his limbs limp and cold. Analee knew Sam's physical strength had been sapped by the nausea and the ordeal, but would his inner strength be enough to see him through the long day ahead?

After giving her order, she quietly prayed that it would...

Buck looked at Kate and said, "Mrs. Mays, how about you? Is there anything Bill can get you before he closes up the kitchen?"

Buck looked at Bill, hoping he'd taken the right tact. The older man nodded his approval, then both looked beseechingly to the grieving widow for an answer. They were disappointed by her reaction, perhaps, but far from surprised.

Kate, still in shock over losing her husband, merely quivered and could not speak.

Buck nodded quietly. Bravely he added his order, hoping his enthusiasm might be contagious and perhaps spark Kate's imagination, "I'd like pancakes and sausage, Bill, with lots of maple syrup, while you're at it why don't you throw in—"

Suddenly, Kate broke from her shell and, in a trembling voice, almost whispered, "Milk, I'd really love a big glass of ice cold milk right now."

One by one, the passengers nodded their approval as the trembling woman spoke. A buoyancy lifted the group; though Hank was lost forever, they'd managed to save one of their own from the abyss. Each pair of eyes met the other; they smiled, nodded, until at last one of them spoke.

Analee, who felt that perhaps she'd been a tad too harsh on Kate earlier, softened her smile and said, "Yes, of course, how could I forget?!?! Milk for me too, Bill. If you'd be so kind!"

The other's rallied in kind: "Me too, Bill. Milk's good for what ails you!"

"Make that two glasses over here, with some of Mom's guava cobbler please," said Sunny.

"One for the road, my good, sir..."

And on and on it went, until at last Bill had filled all of their orders, no matter how imaginary—and elusive—they might have been. Buck nodded silently; glad they had overcome this, at least for now.

Some of them had been resistant at first, he knew but now they seemed relieved to have passed the morning in light instead of darkness. Hank's death had been a sobering wake-up call to all of them, in more ways than one.

Sadly, Buck knew it might not be the last. The human body could go weeks without food, only days without water, but not under the intense conditions the survivors faced as another hot day dawned bright and brutal.

The Captain, Hank, two down, a dozen of them left. Grimly, Buck's eyes moved from face to face. When his eyes settled on poor Lex, still clinging to life but clearly in controlled agony, he realized it was likely the man might not last the day.

From his pained expression, Lex seemed to know it, too…

Despite their forced levity, however, it was clear to Buck that the swimmers were so exhausted, they were barely able to paddle around anymore. He watched them flail in the water, the wives settling lower with their husbands draped around their necks, the men feeling guilty and sad from putting them out.

Buck nodded grimly to himself; this was going to be another long day…

And he had no idea how many of them would be left at its bitter end.

If any…

The dolphins, meanwhile, were always on watch. The people in the water did not realize it, but the dolphins were actually guarding them and preventing the sharks in the area from getting in too close.

As the humans bobbed like bright pink corks, the dolphins swam, ever alert, circling endlessly and only straying to catch a stray fish for sustenance. They were faithful guardians.

Whether the humans knew it or not…

CHAPTER 14

Searching, Hoping, Waiting

As the survivors enjoyed their imaginary breakfast at sea, it was nothing but coffee and donuts for the gathering masses back on the shore. Sleepy little Yankeetown, she of the rickety docks and cheap, live bait had been the designated area for what was fast becoming a coastal search of massive proportions.

The very air itself seemed charged with electricity, feeding off the many rumors from the people that had flocked to the last place any of the survivors had been seen. A smattering of bereft family members stood, solemn and pale, while rescuers both official and civilian bustled about ready to begin the search for the boat and passengers.

Gathering in bunches as strong, loud men barked orders or shouted coordinates, while others started off singly, readying boats and equipment.

The rutted dirt road strewn with broken clam and scallop shells that led to and from the tiny dock was clogged with vehicles of all kinds, from patrol cars from the Ocala Sheriff's Department to the first of the dozens of Coast Guard and state vehicles that would eventually descend upon Yankeetown.

By dawn that Monday morning, the narrow strip of road once rarely traveled suddenly resembled the crowded parking lot at some federal agency. Every available space was filled, until at last incoming cars were directed to park along the narrow road way on either side of the Yankeetown turnoff.

Local residents passing by on their first day back to work after the weekend wondered at the sight. Though Yankeetown was small, not everybody was aware that Sunday' grouper excursion had turned into a problem at sea.

The news couldn't wait long, though; by lunch it was all anybody would be talking about, and like a pilgrimage even more of the community would converge on Yankeetown, eager to lend a helping hand or just pass along a tray full of fresh sandwiches for the searches, and the waiting family members.

All morning men had been pacing the docks, the slips, the road, and even the swampy grassland surrounding Yankeetown, eager to look for those they feared might be holding on for dear life, but none more so than Sheriff John Harris, who had been one of the first to make his way down the uneven road.

Although he had not slept much that night, John was newly invigorated by the hordes of desperate, helpful souls who arrived in the intervening hours between dawn and now. Now the docks were alive as he was, and streaming with would be searchers both young and old, experienced and rookie.

They clustered, waiting for word, whispering premonitions and told wives tales or bolstering each other's sprits with hearty backslaps and kind words. It was part picnic, part madhouse, and like everyone else, John's emotions teetered like a seesaw, depressed and hopeless one minute, confident and optimistic the next.

Like many experienced lawmen, he knew it to be the way of all search parties, be they for tree stuck kittens or teenage runaways. How often he'd stood sentinel over a cooling cup of coffee and crying family, only to get news hours into the search that the missing teen had been found at a friend's house, unaware of the hoopla caused by his or her "disappearance," the cat to be found up a nearby tree on a neighbor's property, mewling happily and content to be the center of attention once again.

So, too, had he experienced the flip side of such searches; the pale, lifeless body of a husband who'd been feared missing after never returning home from work his corpse hanging half-in, half-out of his car's shattered windshield in a ditch.

The families he'd greeted with good news in such situations revered him; those whose doorsteps he'd darkened with grim news and outstretched arms were wary of him. How this particular search would end up was anybody's guess, but Sheriff John Harris was trying his best to remain positive.

He wasn't alone. At last, the Sheriff had finally met the woman who had started it all, Analee's mother Lynn Morgan. His heart went out to the weary, frustrated mother, who had tried her best to rise to the occasion by wearing her Sunday best and arriving at the Yankeetown dock long before any of the others, her hair fixed and her face pale, already long since stained by the streaks of her frequent tears.

They had spoken briefly, and along with his Chief Deputy, Matt McGuire, he helped to fill in the concerned mother about all the hoopla that currently surrounded them.

"I want you to know, Ma'am, that we're doing everything possible to find your daughter and the rest of the group. We've already notified the Coast Guard of the boat's disappearance, and they are now ready to assist in the search.

"My brother Lester Harris is a Florida Highway Patrol radio operator and he'll be keeping track of all the ground, sea and air searches. We needed someone to coordinate the search, to make sure the right hand knows what the let hand is doing, so to speak. He has already radioed Bartow Air Base for additional help, so rest assured we'll have as many eyes in the sky as we'll have on the sea.

"Highway Patrolman Thomas is to stay with the families here at the Yankeetown dock. He's that big man over there in uniform you need anything you let him know. Another patrol sergeant is at the dock at Cedar Key, where some more of the boats are lined up to begin searching.

"I don't want to alarm you, but there's no telling how long the boat has been stranded, if that's what happened. A boat adrift is at the mercy of the sea, in general, and the sea's currents, in particular. By now it could be anywhere, we're not leaving a single cove, inlet, or estuary unsearched.

"I just got off the phone with Lieutenant Trenton at the Coast Guard; he has helped us focus our search efforts on the most likely area where the boat might have been drifted.

"Also, planes from the Coast Guard, stationed at St. Petersburg, are on their way and the Air Sea Rescue Squad and Mac Dill Air Force Base in Tampa, is sending a plane. Plus, the Miami Coast Guard is sending six aircraft and an 83-fott cutter.

"The whole coast is on alert, Ma'am. We'll find them. We've even got local boaters from Yankeetown and Ocala to help out. The sun is up and we're fixing to get started. Not a moment is being wasted, Ma'am. It's a full out search!

"As soon as each group arrives at Yankeetown, they receive instructions on where to begin. They know their job, and they'll do it well. These aren't just lost boaters to them; it could be their family in need of help one day."

The sheriff let his voice trail off, suddenly sapped of energy. He'd been aware of the depth and breadth of the search, had even coordinated most of it, but not until formally relating it to one of the family members did he realize just how big it was.

It wasn't every day cutters from Miami and the Keys sped hundreds of miles to look for a boat lost off sleepy little Yankeetown, but this was no ordinary search. Summer was in full swing, and fourteen civilians were lost at sea. If this wasn't what those hale and hearty Coast Guardsmen were trained to do then what was? Equally as tired as he, Lynn nodded somberly. "Thank you, Sheriff. I'll try to remember all that you've told me, and share it with the other families. I see some of them are already here, I assume the rest will follow shortly."

The Sheriff noticed she spoke almost by rote, and worried that she was already losing hope. He quickly quashed the though, knowing that like him she too was on an emotional roller coaster, one neither of them could get off until the families had been found, for better or worse.

"That would be much appreciated, Ma'am," he said, reaching out to touch her arm. He noticed her eyes well up and he knew if he said much more she might not be able to hold back the tears, she had enough friends and family around, and he was aching to be able to actually do something.

He watched as she walked off, her shiny paten leather pumps out of place on the slippery, uneven planks of the dock. She walked on, her pocketbook in one hand, a fresh handkerchief in the other, as she gathered the half dozen or so family members already assembled to her side. He watched their pained faces as she recounted the news.

"Think we'll find them soon, sir?" asked his Chief Deputy, Matt McGuire.

The sheriff squinted his eyes against the morning sun. "I do, Matt," he said earnestly, stepping aside as several local captains rushed to their boats in order to take full advantage of the rapidly rising sun. "I have to think so, and so do you."

Matt's young face, so innocent and unlined, stared back at the Sheriff with confidence and hope. "I know we'll find them, sir. We have to. Bill's been cutting my hair since I was old enough to sit in his chair. Course, I had to use a phone book or two, but that didn't bother him none."

He smiled warmly, recalling the fond memories of lazy Saturday mornings spent halfway between sleep and excitement, the snip-snip of Bill's scissor creating an unintentional lullaby. "Why, his wife even baked me a cake when she heard I was joining the force," he continued, his mood suddenly growing somber. *Another victim of the search and rescue roller coaster*, the sheriff though ruefully. "I just can't imagine anything bad happening to two people like that. We'll find them, damn it."

As a member of yet another search party interrupted Matt to ask him for a spare canteen, the sheriff nodded absently to his young deputy's back. In his late twenties he was far from an old-timer himself, but he'd seen enough in his day to know that happy endings didn't always happen just because you wanted them to. Sometimes, he knew all too well, bad things happened to good people, even the barber who'd been cutting your hair since you were big enough to sit in his chair.

The morning light deepened, brightening, casting its spell on them all. Slow hours slid by as one by one the dock's slips emptied of their boats, local captains pressing out to sea on full tanks of gas and full stomachs, eager to find the survivors, meaning to stay out until, *success!*

Airplanes from the nearest Air Force bases rumbled overhead, cementing the gravity of their situation with their throttling engines and dipping wings even as their gleaming underbellies bolstered the families' sprits that help was on the way.

The sheriff and his deputy stayed busy coordinating the search, until at last all agencies had reported in and had since shipped out. Just after noon, he and Matt's bellies filled by the heaping cold cut sandwiches and sweet tea donated by a generous local café, the sheriff heard yet another plane rumble overhead. A thought occurred to him.

Using the single, overworked phone at the Yankeetown dock the Sheriff quickly put in a desperate call to Ocala's Mayor, John Marshall Green. As expected, the Mayor was all too eager to help aid in the search.

"Terrible business," he murmured, the gregarious and born politician suddenly at a loss for words as the town sheriff's pleas brought the situation to his doorstep, "terrible business."

"I've thought of everything I can, Mayor," the Sheriff said, keeping his voice low so as not to alert the family members, who had congregated upon Yankeetown in full force by that point and were keeping constant vigil from the dock's shaded area just off the parking area. "Is there anything I've missed?"

"Not at all," said Mayor Green, "but I'm glad you called nonetheless. You put me in mind of a favor I need called in, and there's never been a better time, wouldn't you say?"

John only nodded, until the silence on the other end of the phone reminded him that the Mayor couldn't see him. "Yes sir," he said.

"John, I'm going to close the office for the day. My secretary will be around to take the call if you find anything; she'll know how to reach me. But I've been sitting at this desk all morning drumming my fingers and wishing I could help. Now I know how I can. I'll call you later if I've had any luck."

Quickly disconnecting from his loyal sheriff, Mayor Green immediately dialed the number of an old friend, Chandler Reese, who just happened to own his own plane. "Don't know why I didn't think of this earlier, Reese," said the Mayor, "but I'm deputizing you into being my pilot, if you don't mind."

Far from minding, the local businessman and amateur pilot was more than eager to help out, and told the Mayor to meet him at the local airstrip within the hour. Together the two old friends took to the sky sailing over the local waterways in Chandler's small Piper Cub.

They scoured the shoreline in a futile forty mile search for the missing boat. They looked and looked, but there was no sign of a disabled craft anywhere in the deserted water. They saw nothing but blue skies and the endlessly deep blue sea. They grumbled and groused, eager to keep flying, but the small private plane could only carry so much fuel, and reluctantly the two turned around and headed for home.

Well before the close of the business day, the Mayor was grounded and back at his desk, phoning his Sheriff with the disappointing news and getting some in return: after a morning and afternoon of searching, the Air Force, the Coast Guard, the local captains and his own Sheriff's Department had all come up empty-handed.

The Hazy Days, it seemed, had vanished into thin air…

CHAPTER 15

The Storm Gathers

The life of a captain's wife is no picnic, and no one in Yankeetown knew that better than the long-suffering Lauren Wilson. Her husband, L.B., often liked to joke that he had two wives: Lauren and the sea. (Though not always in that particular order.) Lauren agreed readily, knowing that most days the sea won out, and she was but a poor mistress, waiting at home for her sailor husband.

The butterflies that used to torment her stomach during the early days of her marriage were still there, fluttering upon her waking every morning and slowly disappearing until she rose the next day, only to greet them again.

It wasn't that she doubted L.B. or his capabilities aboard a boat. IT wasn't just wifely pride that found her bragging about her husband's abilities with a boat or a fishing rod; she would have respected his talents whether the two had been perfect strangers and she but a casual observer.

While she was no landlubber, she'd never quite seen anyone so at home on a boat as L. B. Indeed, it was only on shore where she ever saw him insecure or uncertain of his abilities. Like many a sailor, her husband had saltwater running through his veins and was more at home on the deck of his boat than his own front porch or seated around the dinner table.

It wasn't that she and the girls didn't feel his love; L.B. was both an attentive husband and loving father. He just seemed...out of place on dry land; like a fish out of water. Far from clumsy around an anchor or net, he was often bumping into tables or tripping on her well-placed throw rugs, as though unfamiliar in his very own living room.

It was a running joke that while her husband had yet to take a spill into the ocean he'd taken many a tumble on his own front porch! And yet he was beloved by Lauren and his daughters, who welcomed the sight of his perpetually sunburned face, grease stained ball cap or salt spray blasted clothes as he ambled through the front door each night, bringing home a heaping helping of freshly filleted grouper, snapper or pompano.

Of course, his routine was driven by the sea, and on stormy nights she expected him earlier than usual just as on days when the breeze was nonexistent and the sky cloudless, she could expect him home later.

Then there were those rare occasions when, after a particularly late charter, or one that had gone afoul, with too many fish to clean or an unruly group of fisherman who'd left his boat a mess, he slept on board, knowing the quick trip home would be more trouble than it was worth.

Though he'd only done so twice in the six months since he owned the Hazy Days, he'd called home both times. Still, Lauren was realistic. You couldn't very well marry a sailor and then turn right around and expect him to work banker's hours. As she rose that Monday morning to three hungry kids and an empty bed, she simply shook her head knowingly.

Still, after breakfast, she decided that L.B.'s absence was worth commiserating over with Betty Jo Gibbs, Buck's wife and Lauren's close friend and confidante. Buck, being younger and newer married, didn't take his off hours so capriciously. He'd yet to sleep over on the boat, no matter how short his time at home.

Perhaps Betty Jo would fill in the blanks on her missing husband. "Martha," she called, as her middle daughter swung on the front porch swing, desperately bored as the summer dragged on. "Would you mind popping over to the Gilley's house and asking Miss Betty Jo if she's seen your daddy? I fear he's slept on the boat again and I want to know if he needs me to send him lunch!"

Before Martha could answer, she was halfway down the dusty lane making a beeline for the Gibbs residence and thankful for the diversion.

Meanwhile, Betty Jo Gibbs was more worried than her fellow desperate housewife, Lauren. It was, after all, a weekday, and no Buck. He was dutiful about making the quick trip home from Yankeetown after a charter, no matter how early or late the trip might have been. For him not to have arrived home yet, or even called, was unlike her husband.

Fearing only Lauren would be in the know about his tardiness, she sent her own son, Josh, over to the Wilson's to see if there'd simply been a miscommunication of some sort.

Josh, much like Martha, was out the door before his mother could get the words out of her mouth, and had to laugh when he met up with her halfway up the road.

"What are you doing here?" she asked quizzically, as if perhaps Josh was a mind reader.

"I was just about to ask you the same thing" Josh said, scratching his head.

Being children, the two languished in the mid-morning heat, swapping gossip about this tree house or that nephew, unaware of or perhaps even unable to grasp the significance of their missing fathers.

They stood in the middle of the road, scratching mosquito bites or pointing out a particularly colorful lizard or toad. After a few minutes Martha, being the thinker of the two, said, "My mom sent me over to ask your mom where my dad was."

"Me too!" giggled Josh. "I was on my way to your house."

Martha stood with her hand on her hip, something her mother did when *she* was thinking. "Well," she said, "it'll do no good for you to go one way and me the other. We'll just meet in the middle coming back from one another's houses. Let's go to your house and see what your mom says."

"Good idea," shrugged Josh, leading the way.

The children arrived on Betty Jo's doorstep a few minutes later. They were hot and thirsty so she gave them Mason jars full of water while she fretted over what to do.

Martha had no news, and that meant poor Lauren was just as in the dark as she was. A cold dread crept up her spine as she watched Martha, the spitting image of her father, drink her water.

"Martha," she said when the little girl was through. "I want you to go back and get your mother. Tell her to meet me at Yankeetown dock and we'll figure out what's going on with your daddy and Josh's here. I'm afraid it's the only way we're going to get to the bottom of this."

Even Martha could sense the growing panic in Betty Jo's voice. "Are Buck and my daddy okay?" she asked, looking at Josh for support.

Betty Jo, eager to calm the child's fears, put on an air of false joviality and said, "Oh I'm sure they are. You know fishermen; time just gets away from them. I'm sure we'll all be laughing about this by lunchtime, but for now I think its best you run along and fetch your Momma. We'll meet you there, okay?"

Martha shrugged, thanked Betty Jo for the water and, thus refreshed, ran almost all the way home to tell his mother what Buck's wife had suggested.

Lauren was far from comforted by the news, and scrambled to find a babysitter for her restless brood. Locating the neighbor girl, who was glad to help, Lauren grabbed her purse and walked straight down the road to the dock.

Lauren was far from relieved by the tense atmosphere that had gripped Yankeetown since the search started that morning in earnest. Parking much too far away for her taste, she made the last leg of the trip on foot and knew for certain she looked a wreck by the time she parked her car and made it to the Yankeetown dock.

The sight of all those empty slips depressed; some part of her had fully expected to see the Hazy Days languishing there in its regular berth, with Buck and L.B. cleaning up from the party of late fishermen or perhaps making repairs on the boat.

Instead, she found an equally distressed Betty Jo talking to a handsome young man in uniform. The two women rushed to embrace, and before Betty Jo could relate what Sergeant Thomas had just told her he launched in anew, none too eager for the women to begin feeding off of each other's paranoia and fear.

"Mrs. Wilson," he said kindly, looking her in the eye unflinchingly, "I just told Mrs. Gibbs here that, unfortunately, the boat never made it back to shore last night. At his point it's season for concern, but not for panic. We're doing everything we can to find them.

"Believe me when I tell you everyone who can is out there searching for them. We've got the coast Guard coming in from three ports, an aerial reconnaissance plane, a dozen or more local boaters, the sheriff's office, you name them they're out there looking for the boat. I've got reports coming in every hour, and if you'll promise to stick around I'll be more than happy to share whatever news I have with you."

Lauren thanked him, and he pointed to the cluster of family already gathered by the boathouse. "Have a seat in the shade over there, ladies," he suggested, walking them over halfway, "and I promise to let you know the minute I hear something."

The women thanked him and were greeted by none other than Lynn Morgan, Analee's mother, and a frazzled looking Mabel Jennings, Anne and Wanda had picked her up straight up from the drugstore. Upon hearing that both her daughters, Sunny and Ginny, had not come home by that morning. She realized they were late, but she had gone into work, her daughters at home had gotten the phone calls.

The women commiserated, alternately reassuring each other and fueling their panic by expecting the best and fearing the worst.

"Buck and L.B. would never let anything happen to a charter," Betty Jo insisted even as Lauren nodded her agreement. "No doubt the engine stalled and they're sitting out there drifting on the current. If that's the case, they're perfectly safe, if a little sunburned. All they have to do is stretch their bag lunches for a few more hours until they run across the path of one of those Coast Guard cutters."

Mabel clutched her purse, nodding emphatically. "I know Ginny was packing an extra large lunch, and Sunny never made two sandwiches if four would do. I'm sure my girls are entertaining the crowd with stories of their poor, worried mother right about now!"

"I'm sure you are right, Mabel," said Lauren, as eager to sooth her own nerves as those of the other women. "By nightfall we'll all be sitting at Jim's Crab Shack laughing together over how upset we were. Look at that," she said, pointing to the clear blue that surrounded them, "Not a cloud in the sky. I bet they're taking turns cooling off in the ocean and having a good laugh on all of us right about now. They've probably ran out of bait with all that extra time to fish."

"Analee surely loves to swim," said Lynn, finally joining in. "I bet she's teaching Sunny and Ginny the backstroke right about now. L.B. and Buck too, if they know what's good for them!

And so the morning stretched out, hot humid, and sticky. The women shared handkerchiefs, alternating between drying their eyes and cooling the backs of their necks. The boathouse provided little shelter, and all of them stood there, hour after hour, enduing the summer heat as the day wore on.

Any activity caught their eye, from Sheriff Harris gesticulating on his radio to the pelicans floating lazily just off the docks, and so when a lone figure came walking up the dusty dirt road they watched carefully until Lynn Morgan recognized the young woman as Diane, Sam's sister.

Lynn walked out to meet her, giving her an update along the way until soon the six women were seven. "My mother sent me," she explained to the women, wives and mothers all. "She's so worried, she though it better to wait by the phone but we both thought I might be able to find some answers here, but there's been no word?" The women shook their heads in unison. An awkward silence followed until Lacey blurted, "I'm sure Sam is fit to be tied. For him to miss classes like this, so close to graduating, it's not like him. Momma's really worried. Oh here, I almost forgot momma sent sandwiches."

The women thanked her, trying to console the restless young woman, but she was not to be comforted. "Thank you," she said abruptly, before rushing off the same way she'd come. Lynn Morgan frowned, and followed after. They had a brief discussion at the edge of the dock, and then hurried off into the dust, up the unpaved road as quickly as she'd appeared.

"She's gone to get her mother and other family members," Lynn explained, looking worried. "I suppose I can't blame her for her being upset, I feel so helpless, standing around here doing nothing."

Mabel, the oldest one there, cautioned the others that they were doing exactly what they should be doing. "Leave the rescue to the professionals," she warned. "They know what they're doing. When they return, towing in your husband's boat, Lauren, we'll be here waiting, the first thing our family member see. I know it's frustrating to wait, that we all want to do more, but the best we can do is be here when they make it back. And that's exactly what I intend to do."

One by one, the other women nodded, smiling gratefully at Mabel's words of wisdom. If only the rest of Mabel's children could hear them. Fred was at work, but was being informed.

Meanwhile Dolores Jennings, wife of Fred, brother of both Sunny and Ginny, was at Will and Sunny's home relieving poor Betty Jean of her babysitting duties while the other Potter children played quietly together in the living room.

Dolores Jennings was washing the lunch plates when a patrol car pulled into the driveway, his lights not flashing, his siren quiet, but his presence causing the floor to drop out of her very life.

She watched from the kitchen window, a wet plate still dripping in her hands, as a solid, sturdy deputy rose from the car and began walking toward the front door. She met him there, a dishtowel drying her wringing hands, just as he knocked.

She had hoped to cut him off at the pass, but now the children were crowding around and in a grave voice full of clipped tones the deputy explained that the boat was "unaccounted for" and that everything possible was being done to find it. She thanked the deputy and watched him walk away.

She'd already known something was amiss, of course. Dolores knew Will would have been at work for hours by now, if it was at all possible. The younger Potter children, Tony, aged 9, and Jason, aged 3, were unaware of any misgivings; however, Betty Jean was 14, and knew things were not right. She couldn't remember her parents being gone overnight before, and she always helped her mother with breakfast in the summer.

Her parents should be home by now...

Back at the dock the original group of four family members had grown by leaps and bounds. Word around town had spread quickly, and by late afternoon shops had closed early and the sidewalks were rolled up.

Nearly everyone in town knows the captain, the crew, or the passengers, some through family relations, some through church, others through shopping at their stores of simply getting their haircut. Bill Saunders cut the hair of all five of the passengers.

The missing boat is not just big news in Ocala; it's stopped the town in its tracks. Those that haven't already fled to the docks for more news cluster around their radios back home, lighting candles in the window for the boat's safe return or saying an extra prayer as the afternoon drags slowly on.

In the churches, the diners, at the police station and city hall, there is little else to talk about. Old salts share stories of their own trials at sea while calmer heads soothe the minds of local citizens that the boat will pull in soon, either under its own steam or dragged behind a Coast Guard cutter.

At the docks themselves, the families cluster around each other. Now older children have joined the group, no longer able to keep the grim news from reaching their ears and they shift restlessly from one foot to the other, straining their necks for another look out to sea and frowning as, hour after hour, they see little more than open water and the searing rays of a blazing sun. Friends of the missing boaters keep bringing food just in case they were rescued while they were there with some welcome food. The boaters would be very hungry and thirsty after these long hot hours on the water.

CHAPTER 16

Monday in the Water

Buck floated in the water, bobbing up and down while staring at the red rimmed, almost dead eyes of the survivors. Staring at the wan, listless faces dipping perilously close to the water's surface, he saw that indeed "the day was going to be hell."

Emotion was gone, replaced by only the most necessary of bodily functions. Desire had been replaced by doubt, and instinct that taken the place of inspiration. There was little hope left, only the shaky vital signs of a handful of survivors still struggling to stay alive.

The group was beyond sunburned; their skin was now a shiny, almost slick sheen caused by the effects of sun poisoning. Most were in dire need of medical attention, but despite the endless hours without food or water their bodies' soldiered on, instinctively fighting to keep alive despite the grim odds stacked against them.

Lack of water had caused their mouths to close; most of them seemed content to keep it that way. A profound silence permeated the tight-knit circle Buck insisted that they keep. It was a not comfortable silence; speaking took energy and that was in short supply.

They had settled into a harsh reality; a place where manners or kind words or laughter dare not tread. Each was suffering from his or her own personal, private hell. There seemed little need to share it.

The pain they'd so long endured had since shifted from excruciating to unavoidable. It was a part of them, tightly woven into the fabric of their endless suffering. It was no exaggeration; for many of them there truly seemed no end in sight. They'd long since given up on scanning the sky for rescue planes, or straining their necks to crane for the sound of a passing motorboat.

The world was gone; in its place was this circle, these people, their fears, and their pain. IT was all they had; it was all that mattered. As the day passed moments melded into each other; hours could go by in the blink of an eye while seconds seemed unendurable.

They contented themselves, if one could truly call it that, with thoughts of their families, their friends, their homes, their past lives. Faces flashed before them; the smiling, happy, innocent faces of the holiday weekend past.

At some point their grim reverie was intruded upon by the sputtering of one of the group. One by one they shook off their stupor, peeled open their sun-swollen eyes, and stared from face to face, finally settling on Lacey as her lips darted beneath the surface once again, her swollen red nose bright beneath the clear blue water as she struggled with her husband still clinging to her back.

She came back up quickly sputtering and regaining consciousness, her voice constricted by the thirst that haunted them all. "Lex," she gasped, the tremors of her vocal chords almost too painful to endure. Despite the blinding pain she opened her mouth wider to yell, "LEX!"

From her back there was no response. Buck looked quickly to see why Lex might not be responding and found his answer immediately: Lex's face was fully forward in the water. Even with Lacey sputtering wildly for her husband, the man's head remained lolling, face down.

Buck signaled grimly to Bill, who was already climbing off the back of his wife for a better look, together they paddled over to Lacey, Bill calming his family friend while Buck checked the vital signs of her husband.

"Bill," urged Buck quietly so as not to alarm the rest of the group, "help me get Lex off Lacey's back. He isn't able to keep his head out of the water."

The men struggled to shift Lex's dead weight. Both men were tired, and doing anything physical required a heroic act of strength. Their strength had been sapped by the heat, the endurance of paddling for over 24 hours, and the complete and utter lack of either food or water.

As they hefted his sunburned body, they realized Lex had already died, perhaps only a short time earlier. There was no time, nor reason, to keep the secret from his wife. As they struggled to right the man, Lex's dead, lifeless eyes stared back at his wife, as if eager to spare her the woes of false hope. There was no fear of that; Lacey realized the truth right away. She immediately became hysterical; she couldn't believe Lex was dead.

"I didn't feel him leave me," she insisted. The rest of the group nodded, the women paddling closer, Buck and Bill taking advantage of the women's hysteria to quietly let Lex drift soundlessly into the briny blue depths. Involuntarily, Bill crossed himself as the last sight of his old friend vanished forever.

Tearfully Lacey cried, "I should have felt something when he left me. Wouldn't you think so? We were so close. He couldn't have died and left me without my knowing when it happened. How could he do that?"

Her eyes moved from face to face, seeking an answer she would not find. After that, Lacey mourned in private, her chapped, blistered lips moving quietly in silent prayer. The others joined her, praying for poor Lex, for his widow, for each other, for themselves.

Almost as an afterthought, they prayed for rescue...

Faintly, high up and far away from them, the group could hear the distant sound of an airplane motor. They looked at each other, interrupting their prayers in disbelief. Could it be? Was it real? Was this some kind of sign? At long last an answer to their prayers?

Buck hushed their hopeful whispers; silencing them with a menacing look that was all business, and little mercy. The heat had sucked the very noise from the air, the water was still and calm. Even Lacey's moans and gentle tears fell silently. Yes, it was there; faint but strong, quiet but true.

A plane was passing overhead. The hum of a distant engine hovered over them all. It droned on mechanically, a modern thing in this world of clear water and blue sky; glinting, heavenly metal against the endless white clouds.

Suddenly, instinctively, the water churned with activity as reality sped new blood through old veins. Senses awakened and nerves jangled as hope glistened anew. The men waved their arms frantically, feeling the blisters and sores on their back pop and tear, the sting between their flexing should blades a small price to pay for the hope of freedom.

Sunny and Lacey scrambled to get their mirrors out of their handbags. Like Girl Scouts earning a merit badge they angled the compacts into the sun, trying to flash a bright stream of rays toward the airplane.

Despite their efforts, the mirrors, the waving arms, the screams, and then the tears, the plane never strayed from its flight plan. It soared, high overhead, straight and true, until at last even the drone of its engines became but a bittersweet memory.

It had been too high to see the sun's rays filtered through an atmosphere dancing with heat waves and white clouds. The pilots' radio, the rattle and hum of the engine, there had never been a chance that the men's shouts might meet the ears of those flying the plane.

The disappointment was almost unbearable. Only minutes earlier they had been content in their pain, their emotions dead, their hope nonexistent. The plane had changed all that, bringing them up to the mountaintop only to dash them right back down again, only this time lower than before.

Words could no longer express the depths of pain the survivors endured in the wake of the plane's quick arrival and even hastier departure. From his own private place of pain, Will watched the others react with depression and dismay.

He watched Bill and Buck, still treading water, still commiserating over the plane's departure and their vain hopes for its return, and how the women who'd borne their weight all night now floated easily, almost effortlessly, without their burden.

They were choking less and less in salty water, their chins higher, their necks less stiff, their shoulders unburdened. Will's eyes closed tightly; behind their lids he saw his grim future grow shorter and shorter.

His heart told him to let go; for once, his head agreed. He was so tired. Having missed breakfast Sunday morning, a mere oversight in the carefree hours of his former life, now a deadly mistake in this new scenario, he was eight hours hungrier than the other survivors.

His hunger had moved from unpleasantness to annoying to weakening to life-threatening. His body literally had nothing left to feed on. His muscles were cramping as his body fought for fuel; every thump of his heart occurred at the cost of his waning energy.

Sunny, to begin with, wasn't in much better shape. He saw her weakening in front of him, felt her bobbing less and less and sinking more and more. He was aware of hearing her cough, choke, and sputter as she dipped below the surface yet again, her mouth spitting out the deadly salt water that threatened to send each and every one of them to an early grave.

In seconds, he made a choice that would save his wife's life. He realized both he and Sunny might drown, and that neither one might make it home to their kids. Knowing that Sunny was now the stronger of the two, he made a courageous decision.

"Sunny," he whispered hoarsely, "I'm going to let go, honey. I'm too tired to hold on any longer; I'm only weighing you down. With me, we both might die. Without me, you could surely live."

Sunny began to protest, her shoulders arching stubbornly, her head shaking wildly, the salt water clinging to her wet hair whipping against them both.

"Listen," he begged. "You must be the brave one, and live for our kids. I love you."

She began to open her mouth, but Will had already made his decision. Kissing the back of her head fondly, he released both of his hands at the same time, the dead weight of his limp body slipping quickly beneath the surface.

His body reacted with a jerk as Sunny, with a strength surprising even to herself, jerked her husband back up. "NO!" she screamed. "Hang on. I love you. I need you. Our kids need you. We'll make it, Will. We can get through this together!"

Coughing, sputtering, he fought against her vice-like grip. "Let me go," he begged, "let me go."

She fought him, tooth and nail. "You can't leave me, Will," she bargained, trying to guilt him into staying with her. "I'll never be all right without you. I'll never be the same!"

She begged and pleaded for him to just hold on a little while longer. "Please, Will, for me," she cried. He slumped against her hands, shook violently, and strained to be let go of.

The others joined in and pleaded, "Will, don't do this—oh GOD! Don't do this."

Will popped up one last time, looked at Sunny and then, summoning all the inner strength he had, slid beneath the surface for a final time. As soon as the water covered his head, Sunny became hysterical. She yelled, she cursed, she screamed out to God, "Please, no—don't let him go!"

But Will was already gone. He had joined the others in the briny depths, leaving Sunny to carry on without him. She was inconsolable in his absence, unsure about whether or not to follow him. Sensing this, the others came together, circling about, and comforted her.

Crying and ranting with grief, Sunny turned her attention to her sister, Ginny. She hoped to salve her own wounds by focusing on her sister, but too soon realized her sister was in worse shape than she was!

Sadly she thought, "Oh, God, something is wrong with Ginny. Her lips are blue, and her face is swollen." She swam close, hoping for the best and finding the worst. She struggled to keep Ginny's head up, talking to her all the while, quietly telling her how much she loved her.

She got no response.

Sunny looked over at Pete. Even before Will had gone, Pete had seemed lost and in shock. A faraway look marked his gaze; his eyes were too white, too wide, moving too fast for their own good. Sunny tried to get his attention, eager to communicate about Ginny's condition. She hoped that she might be able to reel him in, get him to focus on reality. Instead she quickly realized that, though he seemed stronger and more alert than Ginny, he appeared to be "losing" it rapidly.

Suddenly, he put his hand under the surface and came up with a mouthful of water, telling everyone, "The water is fresh just under the surface. Take a drink." A gasp rippled through the slowly dwindling group of survivors. They gasped to watch Pete drinking from the water as if it were a public fountain in downtown Ocala.

His eyes grew wilder, if that was possible, as he dipped below the surface for another scoop. Before anyone could stop him he gulped down more than his share. Buck and Bill, in concert, tried desperately to get him to stop. They thrashed about in the water, fighting to reach him, but soon his actions became so incomprehensible the two just stopped and stared, unable or unwilling to do more harm than good.

Pete was still talking to Ginny as though she was answering him. All of a sudden he turned to Sunny and asked for a Coca-cola. Before she had a chance to react, pitifully he said to her, "I thought you liked me, but you don't, not really, I know that now. You gave everyone else a Coca-cola, except me."

Sunny was crushed; first Ginny unresponsive now Pete was accusing her of hating him. She stammered, confused, ashamed, guilty, knowing this wasn't true but somehow wondering if perhaps it might be, so she told Pete, "Pete, don't drink the salt water. It's not fresh, it's bad for you. It can kill you, everybody knows that."

Pete was livid, drawing strength from his insanity as he railed at her, "Well, what should I drink? You gave out all of those Coca-Colas even drank the last cold one yourself. Drank it all up. Coca-Cola, Coca-Cola."

Tears flowed down Sunny's face as Pete continued his horrific litany, chanting in his sun and thirst-induced delusion, "Coca-Cola. Coca-Cola. Coca-Cola." For variety he stretched the symbols out, only increasing Sunny's shame. "Cooooo-ca, Cooo-la. Cooo-ca Cooola."

The rest of the group floated on the fringes, in awe of the surreal spectacle as Pete's hallucinations made them fear him, and pity him, all at the same time. They lent Sunny support with their eyes, hoping she might understand that Pete was delusional, that he was not in his right mind, that the grief from

Ginny's coma and the stress of the situation had rendered him, quite literally, senseless.

It mattered not. The strains of Pete's dry, hoarse throat made his taunts even more maniacal. His face contorted with grief, pain, confusion, sadness, flashing over into rage, anger, and accusation.

"How could you drink the last Cooo-ca Cooo-la?" he asked foam and salt water bunching at the corners of his lips as he spewed for more venom: "How could you do this to *us*? How could you do this to *me*? Please, I just want some soda. I know you have some. Please, I beg you, give it to me. Give me some Cooo-ca, Cooola. Give me some Cooo-ca, Cooo-la…"

Pete's accusations at last lost their sting. Sunny focused her energy on her baby sister instead. Ginny, she realized, was really out of it now. Nothing verbal was coming from her lips. When Sunny attempted to lift her head, Ginny's lolled back on the life vest, making her appear doll-like and lifeless. Meanwhile, Pete was talking to her as if she was fully awake and carrying on a conversation with him.

"We'll have some Coca-Cola when we get home, honey. And we won't share any with Sunny. What do you think about that?"

Finally, Sunny realized that her baby sister, Ginny, was dead, even though Pete was still talking to her like she was alive. She also realized that Ginny's floatation device was needed, so she tried to get Pete away from Ginny. She realized in his state that he would never see the uselessness of letting Ginny's body float while others could benefit from the vest.

Sunny looked to Buck, who silently understood the need to remove Ginny's vest.

Finally, when Pete turned his back and was talking to the others, still trying to convince them that the salt water was "delicious," Sunny was at last able to untie the strings with stiff fingers and ease Ginny out of the vest.

Pete's condition allowed him to see what he wanted to, he saw that his wife had no vest on and that Sunny was still holding on to her. He continued to talk to Ginny as if she was alert and responsive. Buck gave the jacket to Sam, the worse off of all the remaining passengers.

The minutes passed in agony; the rest of the group silent while Pete rattled on. His love for Ginny was evident; so too was the fact that he was fast losing his grip on reality. In one sentence he'd be babbling on about how great the water was, in the next he'd be making plans for Christmas.

His energy was inexhaustible; he never...stopped...talking. After an hour or so, Sunny talked to her dead sister, told her she was so sorry; but she wasn't strong enough to hold on to her any longer.

Timidly she asked her sister, "Ginny, please don't be mad at me. I tried to hold on as long as I could. I really wanted to take you home to Momma." Sunny cried, and everyone else was whimpering and crying, too. However, no tears would come.

They were all simply too dehydrated.

Sunny reluctantly let Ginny go. She slipped into the water with only a soft wet sound. One they had all become increasingly familiar with of late. Pete realized what was happening as he saw Ginny disappear under the water. He screamed at Sunny, "Why did you let her go?"

He started thrashing and calling, "Wait! Ginny! Baby!"

He dove under, came up once, calling Ginny's name the whole while, his face coated with the salty brine, his lips bathing in it, his words clouded by it. He dove again and came up once more, saying, "Hold on, Sweetheart, I'm coming."

"He gave a big yell, then dove in once again. In his weakened state his mind was too weak to help him as he grappled with an invisible demon. With the other survivors waiting, watching, powerless to help, he did not resurface. He and Ginny sank slowly down...

Much smaller now, the group realized it was only going to get worse...

"Lees," said Sam in a croaky, scratchy voice, almost a whisper, "I am so sorry, this is all my fault you came with me on this trip, and I don't think I will make it home. I want to tell you goodbye before its too late."

"Oh no you don't, Sam," She replied in a desperate sounding plea. "You will not leave me! You are hanging on! I chose to go on this trip. It is not anyone's fault. It was an accident. We are going to be rescued. Don't think we won't. I don't want to say goodbye. I just won't do it. You hang on, damn it, Sam. Do you hear me???" She said again, "do you hear me???"

CHAPTER 17

A Squall

During the search on Monday afternoon, a severe squall developed, affecting the rescue. Many boats are forced to drop anchor six miles out. The squall does not let up, and gets even worse. The sky is very dark. This weather sends the men below deck to stay dry and out of the lightning that is crashing nearby. The worse they'd all been expecting came quickly and without warning. The squall moved in from the east, blocking out the afternoon sky and grew more ominous by the moment. The blotting out of the sun had an immediate affect: for once the survivors could glance up from their downcast expressions, and not fear the blinding light of its rays.

There was some collateral benefit as well: in a matter of minutes the temperature dropped from well above 90 degrees to a mere 70, but for the wary group they knew any advantage they gained was but a wolf in sheep's clothing, waiting to lure them into submission only to attack them with some unexpected, but grim, surprise later on. Buck issued orders as the wind picked up, "Looks like a squall is coming," he spat, the whitecaps already cresting on top of the wind-whipped waves and throwing water into his blistered face, "if we're not careful, it could tear us apart, send us to all corners of this big ocean."

"What'll we do?" asked Analee over the howling wind, still coherent and trying her best to keep her ailing boyfriend Sam afloat.

"How will we all stay together? Tell us what to do!"

Buck nodded in response to her question, relieved to see that she was still coherent. *Was it her youth keeping her alive,* he wondered silently as he stared at the grim mask of determination that had settled onto her face, *or her faith?* He realized it didn't matter; survival was survival, no matter what the cause.

"Stay together is right!" He answered, still nodding and swimming closer to the bewildered group as the wind threatened to toss his answer in the opposite direction. "We've got to close ranks, get closer to each other, hold hands if we must but if you think this is bad," he paused as a howling gale threatened to blow them apart even as he spoke, "I've seen it get lots worse."

The group, such as it was, did as they were told. Even so, the seas grew rougher and wind blew harder. It seemed the elements would show them no mercy. Though they'd prayed for rain, begged for it, in fact, now that it was here they realized too late the old adage, "be careful what you wish for."

The sun had been blistering, unforgiving, and cruel, but at least the seas had been gentle and calm for the most part. As morbid as it sounded, those who had died had left behind life-saving vests, so that now most of the group could save the effort of dog-paddling and simply float there, up and down on the churning water.

Now all that had changed. In moments the sea had grown angry, riling itself up into a living thing, seemingly intent on seeing them all dashed to the ocean floor, the sooner the better. Now it was a fight just to stay above the water's surface, and legs little used were now put to good use as they kicked just to keep from being overtaken by the vicious, looming swells.

Some were luckier than others. In the water, Lois and Bill were trying to keep their mouths from filling with the roiling salt water. Even though the waves were high, and the lightning and thunder was crashing loudly and close to them, the rains had not yet started. They had been praying for rain, praying so hard for such a long time.

Still that sweet relief eluded them…hours and hours of choppy water with not a drop of rain. At least the sun had gone down, giving them some relief, but for Lois, the reprieve had come too late. She went so quietly, Bill never knew exactly when it happened. One minute he was holding her and talking. God knows what he had been talking about, the kids, maybe, or what they'd do when they got back. But now, there was nothing, no answer, no shy smile, nothing. For Lois, there would be no going back…her head lolled to one side, her eyes lifeless, her lips cold and blue. His heart broke; eyes growing blank as his features froze into a mask of mourning. Even though he knew she was gone, he talked to her, "Goodbye, Honey. I'm so sorry I never should have made you come. Please forgive me."

A reverent silence fell over the group as they struggled to hear a husband's last respects to his wife. Undeterred by the howling gale, Bill continued whispering as though Lois could hear him as she lay, slumped in her life vest, tossed to and fro by the growing violence of the angry sea, "I'll miss you so much. I don't know how I'll make it without you."

Wind whipped the tears from his face so that he didn't have to wipe them away for himself. "I'll take care of our children, darling. I don't want you to worry about them. They're so young, they never got to know you the way I do, but I'll tell them about you every day, dear. I mean that. A day won't pass that I won't tell them how beautiful you were, how talented, how wonderful, how special. They won't forget you. I *won't* let them! I won't forget you, either. Never. And I'll see you in Heaven…"

Buck prayed grimly, his lips moving silently along with the rest of the group. Then he swam over to Bill, and helped him take her out of the life vest. They then decided to put Bill in the jacket. Bill tried to protest, but he was too weak; at last, and with much urging from a still stubborn group, he relented and allowed himself to be assisted into the vest.

Analee watched the process with a heavy heart, and even heavier limbs. Her arms were so tired; she had been trying to shield them with her blouse, so wisely taken off on the deck of the ship. She had thought it silly at the time, and regretted the decision until their fourth or fifth hour in the water, when at last the shirt had been used as a shield from the blistering, unrelenting sun. Now her arms were tired of holding it up, and it seemed useless to keep it any longer. It was obvious to the bright young woman that their situation was dire, and with the storm making the skies overcast and the rain threatening, with the night coming and the sun at last going down, she was sure the shirt would no longer be needed.

At last she took it from her head, and began to let it float away, but just then a flash of lightning illuminated something on the shirt, making her reach for it and drag it back. *What could it be?* She thought as she fought the increasingly violent waves to drag the shirt back. *A button? A needle? Something they might use?* But no, it was Sam's fraternity pin, pledged to her so innocently, so bravely, so sweetly that very weekend. Had it only been a few days earlier that they'd expressed their love for one another, exemplified in this simple pin?

How life had changed since then; how many lives had been lost since then. How angry she would have been to lose such a precious keepsake, when others had fought mercilessly to keep purses above their heads, dry and out of the water, if only to save a few precious snapshots or baby pictures.

Her heart pounded; shamed that she might have cast it aside so capriciously. Holding the blouse close, she kissed the pin and made a decision. Yes, she would keep it and continue using it for shade.

CHAPTER 18

At the Dock

At last the squall ended. Later that Monday, many relatives crowded the dock at Yankeetown looking for news, company, solace, or all of the above. The weather had not kept them away: they'd huddled together under trees, the rickety porch awning, under evening newspapers and ponchos from the neighboring police officers, all to no avail.

The words "drowned rats" might have been appropriate to describe them, though no one had poor enough taste to utter them aloud. Instead they endured their vigil quietly, close-knit because of the storm but miles away in their own heads, mourning in private, heads bent in prayer.

After the rain came the damp, stale humidity. Steam rose from the dock in waves, a sickening, cloying presence that enveloped you like a warm bowl of soup. The storm had at last stopped, but now it seemed they'd only traded one form of precipitation in for another. At least the sun had set, though the reprieve from the sun brought with it a mixed blessing; how scared their family members must have been in the dark, out there on the water, drifting who knew where.

They shrugged off the thought, facing the night with stiff chins and shoulders upright. Since there was only a single overhead light bulb on the shabby boathouse, a couple of nearby residents had thought to bring those assembled for the vigil two or three oil lanterns for the waiting men and women to use after dark.

They'd all stood still during the storm, knowing the survivors must be taking a beating, knowing the rescue boats would be idle until the storm let up; now it seemed as if they couldn't be active enough!

Cold drinks and how coffee in big pots and sandwiches were also brought down to the dock to try to give some comfort to the worried families, as well as to fortify the brave men who'd been searching all day long. They ate ravenously, gratefully, bending to say a quick grace before devouring as much as they could. Somehow, they sensed it was going to be a *very* long night....

Almost simultaneously, all the relatives of the survivors decided to spend the night on the dock until their "children" returned. It was a maternal instinct, no matter what the relation. Each of the passengers had a mother or other caring relative standing on that dock waiting for word of their welfare; no way were they going anywhere until they heard something definitive.

Every few minutes you would hear someone praying for the safe return of their loved ones. Occasionally a mother, daughter, sister, neighbor, brother, uncle, aunt, or friend would step out of the lantern light and into the darkness. Their disappearance was no mystery; although you could no longer see them you could easily hear their sniffling in the dark.

Soon they would appear, red-eyed and apologetic, to join the prayer circle yet again. In the hot, humid summer night, the mosquitoes were swarming so thickly, the distraught people leaned against the boathouse and covered their heads with blankets or anything they could find to stop from being eaten alive.

Nothing worked; you could cover you head but they'd bite your hands. You could cover your hands but they'd bite your face. It was the worst kind of torture, endless and annoying, but none of the family members left their post. Whatever they were enduring might have been bad, they all knew, but nowhere near as bad as what their loved ones had been through and, sadly, were still enduring.

As down broke, they heard a faint "toot, toot" sound coming from the mist-covered water. Almost in unison they stood at attention; none of them had slept. They craned their necks as one, a group moving on pinion legs to get a better sight as a bow pushed slowly through the mist.

"Listen," someone shouted, "it's the tug boat. They must have found them!" Shouts of joy slowly turned to tears of anguish, however, as they soon realized there was only a single boat; their loved ones were not in tow, after all.

It was the Mere-Maid, tooting forlornly, almost apologetically, as if the ship itself regretted returning to port before the survivors could be rescued. The men on board shook their heads sadly at the waiting relatives; no words were needed for the depressing verdict. The group, mostly women, at last began to sob in earnest. There was no longer any need to hide one's face or step away for the sake of politeness; pain and tragedy had at last trumped good manners and decorum. Now the women stood, shoulder to shoulder, some leaning, some upright, others borrowing-or lending-a spare handkerchief.

The town's people, who had heard the tug boat, also thought the boaters had been rescued, and they rushed to the dock en masse, a townspeople bolstered by the thought of good news to greet the morning. It was a short-lived and ironic celebration. In the crowd was the local pastor, Bob Hovey. He'd been waiting at the dock, prepared to comfort the family but hoped to rejoice with them. His prayers for the families had been endless, but he had hoped that the tug boat would bring good news and make his presence there the comfort they needed. Now he watched the face of the crowd, he knew they were trying hard to keep a stiff upper lip, but saw that resolve crumble, smile by smile, tear by tear, and he stepped into the fray willingly, if not confidently.

"Folks," he said quietly but firmly, addressing the mothers and relatives of the survivors, "let's gather if we may and pray for our missing loved ones."

His forced smile masked a concern that went beyond his role as a pastor for a local church. He knew these men and women personally, both on the boat and on the Yankeetown Dock. He'd presided at their weddings and baptisms, he'd been there for them when they were up and when they were down. He knew the Lord would watch over those who'd gone out on the boat that weekend, but while he was busy; Pastor Hovey could certainly do his part on the dock, leading the crowd in prayer and holding their hands as they trembled, then cried.

Bob's wife, Dail, took off when his impromptu prayer vigil trailed off. They often worked in tandem, reading each other's needs. Sometimes Pastor Hovey's firm but gentle touch was the right cause of action, other times Dail's feminine sense of compassion and fun was just the ticket. In this case, Dail felt the need for action to take the women's minds off of their missing family members. Quickly she called out to some of the women in the crowd, "Mildred, Jayne, Sue, let's get these poor dears up to our house for coffee and breakfast. The deputy will let us know if something happens." The people followed slowly, and Sergeant Thomas maintained his lonely vigil for the boaters. Part of him was almost relieved at their departure. Their pain had overwhelmed him, making it hard to concentrate on the next plan of action. For them, it was the end of a long, sad, lonely night. For him, it was the dawn of a brand new day, after a night's rest, a new shift. What should he do next? What *could* he do? He didn't have long to ponder the question; after a quick breakfast and some hot coffee, the group returned to the dock en masse. Forcing a grim smile to his lips, Sergeant Thomas told them he was sorry but he had yet to hear any news. They nodded in unison, until one woman stepped forward with a covered plate. Smiling, she pulled away a napkin to reveal a breakfast of ham and biscuits they'd brought just for him. It would probably be the only real meal he would get that day. Hot coffee was produced and handed over; bringing the only smile of the morning.

CHAPTER 19

Dividing the Group

Buck stared out at the group with a heavy heart and even more leaden expression; they had been, quite literally, cut in half. From the fourteen brave souls that had gone into the water, only seven now remained. There were Buck and Bill, the strongest of the group and, by rights, their unspoken leaders. Then there were Analee and Sam, the young lovers who were still hanging in there. Kate, Lacey, and Sunny rounded out the ragtag group, each woman on the verge of her own private meltdown.

Buck could see it in their eyes, so white and wide and rimmed with the red of tears that would not come. The group was beyond hysteria; they had been through an ordeal most couldn't survive. "Shoot," mused Buck as he tried to fight the irony that threatened to overtake him, "most *hadn't* survived."

There was no food, no water, and worst of all, no rest for two days. They might have been prisoners of war, enduring the harshest of tortures for some unseen master plan. Instead, they were merely victims of fate; an engine past her prime, a crew in over their heads. Meanwhile, the blistering sun had taken its toll, leaving behind several cases of heat stroke and a rash of blisters so big they threatened to eclipse the survivor's many bites and scratches of every kind, from countless crabs to tiny needlefish.

Buck had been jokingly referring to himself and the others as "overcooked lobsters" for the past 24 hours. The comparison wasn't far off; by now they were all red and covered with hard, oozing bumps of all sizes and descriptions. Their eyes were wild with thirst, fear, emotion, and delirium. Despite his years on the sea, this was nonetheless Buck's first survival story. He'd heard plenty of other, though, and he knew the limits of grown men and women. There was no doubt about it; they had been faced with their limit some time ago, and now were well beyond whatever man was meant to endure. He didn't need the shopworn tales of a dozen old salts back at the Yankeetown dock to tell him what his eyes, his heart, and his gut already could: if help didn't come soon, they'd all be lost.

The young, the old, the men, the women alike, were all equal in the face of nature's fury. It didn't play favorites, if you were unlucky to get in it's way, as these unfortunate seven were, then God help you...by now, He was the only one that could....

Buck signed, splashing his face with salt water and luxuriating in the relative coolness the quick dip provided him. It was all too fleeting; too soon the searing heat of the sun returned, nearly blinding him as he clenched his face against the oppressive white light. He opened his eyes at last, blinked back the salt, and tried to get his bearings. They had drifted constantly since diving off the boat two days ago. He thought he might know where they were, but stilled his beating heart against the hope that it might improve their situation in any significant way. In fact, the more he considered his bearings, the more Buck was sure he knew of a "small island" only a few miles away. Buck planned to take Sam, even though Sam was weakened, Kate and Analee, to swim for shore. It would take a monumental feat to shift from floating to actively moving oneself forward through the warm, turgid waters. These were the only two, besides himself and Bill, of course, who might possibly survive the ordeal. Both were normally strong swimmers, young and resistant so far. Sam was in worse shape than Analee was, but somehow he fought on, resisting the urge to lapse into the sea and time and time again finding the intestinal fortitude to soldier on. Buck felt confident they could make the journey in one piece, if not entirely unscathed. Even better, they could assist Kate, who was clearly not doing well.

Buck made his decision, and call Bill over to tell him of his plan.

"It sounds good to me, Buck," said Bill, steeling himself against his better judgment and nodding more energetically than he had intended. "But let's do it quick; the sooner we start moving, the less chance we'll have to reconsider."

"Good idea," said Buck, turning his attention toward the group. "Gang?" he asked in a voice that left no doubt; he wasn't asking, he was telling. "Bill and I have been talking and we think it's time to split up."

Buck and Bill nodded grimly toward each other as the mumbling started. Buck listened to the water drip from his hand as he lifted it out of the water to still the half-hearted and heat-drenched resistance.

"I know what you're thinking," he continued gamely, not giving the other survivors time to raise objections over his own convictions, "but it's the only way. We've been drifting this whole while, and I'm thinking that we're nearing a small island I'm familiar with." He pointed in a southeasterly direction, getting the group's attention and finally breathing a sigh of relief. "There's an island a few miles over there. At least, if I remember right, I *think* there's an island a few miles over there. I make no promises. Still, if I'm right, at least there'd be dry land beneath our feet, and perhaps clean water. If I'm right, and it's a big "if", that means there's land in the direction we're heading, too.

"What I'm suggesting is that we split up. I'll take a group of the strongest swimmers with me. Sam? Analee? Believe it or not, that's you. We will take turns helping Kate. Bill, Sunny, and Lacey, you will continue floating until you reach land. If either of us gets to shore first, we'll get help for the others. I'm sorry, I just can't see as there's any other way."

Bill noticed the grumbling and thought a familiar voice might help reassure his friends. "He's right," he insisted, slapping the water insistently for emphasis. "It may be easier staying together, but look where that's gotten us so far. We'll still be together; the minute one of the groups finds land we'll alert the others. It just plain makes sense. Gang? What do y'all think?"

Bill and Buck eyed each other as the group discussed it. Slowly, Kate and Analee swam over to Buck, pulling Sam in their wake, his head lolling against the waterlogged life vest as they tried to keep his head above water. No words were spoken; they merely nodded their consent.

The decision was not so easy for the rest of the group: Sunny and Lacey were dead set against splitting up, but had no better idea about how to save their lives. They waffled for a few minutes, but at last shrugged and swam closer to Bill, signifying their agreement all the while their faces screaming that it was "under protest."

Lacey, still distraught after the loss of her husband, waffled back and forth over what to do. Bill and Sunny watched as the emotions clouded her face. She treaded water, caught halfway between the two groups. Finally she said, "Lex always made all the family decisions. I don't know what I should do, or who I should go with. Why is this all so hard?"

"Lacey," argued Bill, understanding all too well her intense pain and confusion but nonetheless pleading his case for her own good, "You're in no shape to swim what may possibly be more than a few miles just in case an island is there. Sam and Analee already have Kate to worry about, and Buck will be focusing his energies on navigating the entire group. It will be much safer with us."

"He's right, Lacey," Buck agreed. Next to him, Sam and Analee nodded their heads vigorously while Kate watched helplessly, torn between leaving her friends and the chance of survival. It took a long while to untie the vests.

At the last minute, however, Lacey decided to go with Buck and the "stronger" swimmers. She apologized profusely to Bill and Sunny, even as she swam ever closer to Sam and Analee, who reached out to her with heavy hearts and bittersweet emotions. Bill and Sunny said they would continue heading in a direction that Bill thought would lead to land. Each hugged the other and said, "Please, if you get rescued, send help for us, too."

Both groups were clearly exhausted, and drifted inevitably apart as their emotions of regret kept causing them to look behind them. There were plenty of tears to go around, and above the sniffling Buck and Bill struggled to keep their respective groups positive about their outlook. They'd began swimming away from each other for several minutes when Lacey, changing her mind yet again, left the larger group with even more misgivings than before. Buck and the others tried to get her to stay, now that the two groups were so far apart for fear that she might get trapped in the no man's land between both groups. There was no hope of success; stubbornly, she started toward Bill and Sunny undeterred.

In their path the water rippled with the slicing fins of their friends, the dolphins. Much like the humans, the crafty mammals had likewise split up from their close-knit pod and decided to stay with the two groups.

Lacey, not really able to see Sunny and Bill, nevertheless kicked and paddled in their general direction. Her mind ran the gamut of emotions as she struggled ever onward and halfway between the two groups she wondered if she'd made the right decision. A bump-what what that. Something was pushing at Lacey, her life jacket was so water logged that her face and mouth went underwater. There was a jolt-something had bumped her leg. Oh GOD! What is it?! Lacey was crying and screaming when up beside her came a huge ugly green sea turtle. She was as frightened of it as she could be. Never having seen one up close, it was horrible. The turtle sort of turned a little and started back down. Oh my GOD! Her long string tie on her vest had gotten tangled on his flipper. He took her under with her screaming. She was swallowing great mouthfuls of water. In a very few seconds the tie slid off of the turtle's flipper, and Lacey was able to surface, but she had taken in too much water and could not breathe.

Her head was lolling in the sea. Lacey was done. She had just drowned and now was just floating barely above water.

CHAPTER 20

Flashback to Family Picnic

Sunny and Bill had been pushing themselves to move toward what they hoped would be land. She was so exhausted. So beaten, so tired. Sunny knew her mind was drifting and worse yet, she was sure that she was dying. She could not catch her breath; the heat sucked the energy from her and her body could not replenish it.

She couldn't remember the last time she'd missed a meal, yet now she'd missed several days' worth. It wasn't the hunger that was slowly driving her mad, though, it was the raging thirst that threatened to dry up her sanity until it withered away and left her unprotected against the ravages of Mother Nature. Her throat felt like it was filled with the hottest sand; simply swallowing was an act of heroism in and of itself.

Suddenly, flashing back to the family picnic, she could almost feel the shade from the huge oaks in her Momma's backyard. Listening to the children playing, she also heard sounds of horseshoes in the background from Uncle Bobby and Uncle Terry. The clang was a familiar, pleasant echo, overshadowing the more realistic and dreadful sound of splashing and flailing as she had watched while Lacey tried to reach the others after they had split up. Hours passed, broiling hot sun, terrible thirst.

There was a moment where she hung there, suspended between the world of the now and the land of the then. The heat withered her, the splashing disturbed her, Bill's breathing, harsh and ragged, serenaded her as they struggled onward toward dry land. And then, just as strongly, she felt the pull of the ever after.

It was powerful and strong. She'd always thought of herself as cool and in control. She'd never been a daydreamer or one for fantasies. She had always felt confident that, no matter what happened her mind would never fail her.

So what was she to think of the backyard mirage that floated just within her field of vision? As her mind drifted, she felt as if her body was cool again, something she hadn't felt for days. Stranger still, she felt…someone…hugging her. She looked over her shoulder, then over to the swing, where once again she sat with her wonderful Will. He was the greatest husband ever. He was rubbing her shoulders softly, her sunburn was gone-and murmuring soothing words.

"Where have you been?" He asked her, but she was in no rush to answer him. She wanted to hear him talk; was desperate, in fact, to hear the soothing sounds of his voice. "I've missed you," he continued, the sound of his voice intoxicating. "I've missed you so badly. Don't ever scare me like that again. I don't want to be alone.…" I am here for you. Come to me.

She was so comfortable and peaceful; she never wanted to leave.

Then there was a shout, from somewhere off in the distance, breaking her out of her reverie: "Sunny, Sunny, for God's sake, don't leave me alone here. Wake up! There are sharks!"

Sharks, no, she did not just hear that, did she? Well, why would there be sharks at a family picnic? And who was that man shouting at her? And why was he interrupting her peaceful talk with Will?

She thought, "I simply will not listen. That will show him."

But the man kept shouting, unwilling-or perhaps unable-to allow her to enjoy her quiet reverie. Suddenly the worlds merged, and past met the present, and she was in the water again, splashing and flailing.

She told Bill, who she barely recognized out of the corner of her eye, "Bill, leave me alone. I'm home with my family."

Awakened by Bill tugging on her, she opened her eyes to see a large shark fin closing in on them. Fear gripped her; she was frozen with the weight of it. She was unable to scream because of her dry throat. Amazingly, Sunny discovered that she and Bill were walking in chest deep water.

Seemingly frozen in place, unable, too tired, and too weak to move, except inches at a time, she knew this was the end. The fin swam closer, and closer. She could feel the evil rippling off of it in waves. She sighed, and stood resolutely to accept her fate.

At least she would be with Will once again.…

All of a sudden several dolphins converged and repeatedly hit the shark in the side until it left. Her sigh of relief was short-lived as she heard Bill's anguished voice once again interrupt her pleasant escape.

"Sunny, stay with me," Bill begged. As she opened her eyes, she saw a huge fin cut the water in front of her about twenty feet away. Then there were lots of fins-smaller and very quick. It was the dolphins coming back to help. "Thank God," she and Bill said together, only to discover that they were not alone.

"Hello?" came and unrecognizable voice, and for once Sunny looked to Bill for confirmation.

Was she hearing things?-she wondered.

The confused look on his face-the way he craned his neck in the water and stared off at a distant spot on the horizon-she thought the ghosts that had come to haunt her were visiting themselves on Bill, as well.

"Are you folks alright?" Came the voice. "Hold on, I'll be right there."

The sound of an outboard motor sputtered toward them as they leaped into each other's arms. Could all their shouting have signaled a rescue? Had their near death experience been, in fact, their salvation?

They thought, "Can it be? Is it a rescue? Is the man real?"

Sunny squinted into the distance. This was no mirage; no backyard barbecue from the past filled with ghosts of people she might never see again. For once the sun illuminated more than mere pain and misery; at last it shone down on the sweet bliss of relief.

Sunny croaked, "Yes, it is a real man and a real boat."

At last, a rescuer had found them.

Or had he?!?

CHAPTER 21

A Bittersweet Rescue

The image seen by Bill and Sunny was no mirage. There was, in fact, a small flat-bottomed johnboat just a short distance away from where they stood. Its exterior was as weathered as its captain; all flaky paint and sad lines, a pitiful but welcome skiff to appear as their own personal knight in shining armor.

The closer it got, the worse it looked. The two survivors could not have cared less. To them, the putt-putting of its tiny outboard engine and the slap-slapping of small, tight waves against its dinged bow were as intoxicating as the trumpet of the Archangel Gabriel himself.

As he sped toward them an old man was hollering out, "Hey, do y'all need any help?" In a slow slurred drawl.

In better circumstances, the two might have shared a laugh. Did they need help?!? As it was, the irony of the old skipper's question eluded them. As dry as their lips were, they were somehow able to croak out, "Yes, yes, over here."

Waving their arms, it seemed, was out of question. Inch by inch, the old captain steered the battered watercraft over to the odd-looking pair. They truly were a sight to behold: Bill in only his shorts and Sunny was wearing only a sundress and a bra, having lost her underwear along the way. It was a testimony to their resilience, not to mention their exhaustion that such normally old-fashioned people cared little about their appearance in the eyes of this new stranger.

Seeing the light at the end of the tunnel was almost as excruciating as not seeing the tunnel in the first place. Suddenly the sun seemed brighter, the water saltier, their thirst greater, their hunger overwhelming. Every crunch of sandy shell beneath their feet felt like daggers upon their soles. They shuffled from foot to foot as the johnboat finally pulled up alongside their red, blistered, battered bodies.

The stranger croaked out a greeting, as if he too was a sun-scorched survivor. "Name's Bud Collier," he said, raising a shriveled old hand. The two didn't notice his sweaty armpits and grease-stained ball cap, which rested on a grizzled, bullet-shaped head. The old man's eyes were wet and rheumy but all they saw was a man-and a boat! He saw an opportunity when one presented itself and wasted no time in continuing.

"What in tarnation?" he asked the bedraggled pair, whose eyes were starting to glaze over by then. "You folks need some help? Well, not to worry; old Bud is here to save the day. All your troubles are over, yesirree indeedy. I am here to help. You just climb on up in the boat here and we'll get you fixed up right quickly I imagine...."

His voice trailed off into a series of guttural grunts as he assisted the badly sunburned Bill and weakening Sunny into the boat. "I was out fishing all afternoon," the old man continued as Bill and Sunny righted themselves in the front of the boat. "I saw you a few minutes ago, truth be told, but I thought you was just a few pelicans flopping about until I saw you moving around. Then I heard some shouting and knew you weren't birds after all."

As the skipper finished his story and choked his engine to life with the pull of a salt-encrusted old rope, the johnboat sprung to attention and buzzed across the flats with a sudden jolt. Bill, the more alert of the two, notice what looked to him to be a small mason jar with water and a small, almost empty, half-pint bottle of gin.

There was something skittish about the old man. Bill took one look at Sunny and know she wasn't long for this world, but Bud seemed unfazed by the entire event. The half-empty gin bottle explained some of that, but it wasn't the drinking that made Bill leery; it was the vacant look in the old salt's eyes...he wasn't acting much like a rescuer.

Bill cleared his throat and pointed to the two bottles, as if perhaps seeing them for the first time. "Are one of those water?" he asked pointedly across the razor blade sharpness of his ravaged throat.

"Yup," Bud said nonchalantly, as if he was quite used to near naked men and half-naked women to and from the marshy flats all day. He had barely glanced at the two since helping them aboard. Instead he kept both hands firmly clasped on the handle of his motor and his head aimed straight at a small landmass growing bigger as johnboat and salty piece of land closed the gap between each other. "Help yourself. There's gin, too, if you're so inclined. Although I'd ask that you save me some, if you don't mind."

Bill's hands trembled with disbelief as he fumbled with the rusty mason jar lid. By now Sunny was nearly comatose, collapsed in a heap in the flat-bottomed slowly-moving johnboat. Bill nudged her and holding up the jar of water and explaining gently, "You can only take small sips, Sunny. I know you'll want more, maybe the whole jug if you could, but you have to control yourself, you'd just throw it up. Here, Sunny, open your mouth and take a drink."

Parting her lips was sheer agony. Despite its high salt content and inherent danger, the ocean water had at least kept Sunny's mouth lubricated from the constant bobbing of her face under the surface. Now, still baking under the heat but without the water's protection, her lips were nearly seared shut.

With great difficulty she swallowed several large gulps before Bill firmly forced the rim of the jar from her cracked, bleeding lips. He noticed the faintest trail of pink on the water's surface but hardly paused as he upended the rest of the jar into his own blistered mouth. Warm, stale water had never tasted so good.... Soon the water jug was empty and Sunny had passed out yet again. Her long wet hair had dried in a matter of minutes and now framed her cherubic, if sunburned, face. Tears sprang to Bill's eyes as he recalled all that they'd been through, to say nothing of the lives that had been lost.

This close to survival, he could think only of those who weren't so fortunate....

Sunny, at least, had made it. If he did nothing else this day, he would see that she made it to the end. As Bill gently took hold of Sunny's hands-half to feel for a pulse, half to seek solace in the warmth of his friend-Bud steered his battered watercraft to a small oyster shell island, where he explained that he was the caretaker.

"I come out from time to time," the old man elaborated, "shoo off squatters or gig me some crabs if they're brave enough to wander too close to shore. Ain't no work to it, and it pays the bills." Bill wondered why anyone would want the small pit of land protected. There was only a small fishing shack, but to Bill's relief Bud pointed out that it had two bunks inside. Bill had never been so happy to see a fishing shack in all his life!

Bud ran the johnboat aground but Bill and Sunny barely felt the jolt as the surprisingly solid craft slowed to a stop. Before it had come to rest, Bill mustered what would amount to the last of his physical strength and had stepped to shore, his feet landing on the prickly spines of thousands of crushed oyster shells which pierced the tender skin of his long-exposed soles.

It mattered little; he reached down and scooped Sunny up in his arms, trying in vain to carry her all the way to the nearby shack before stumbling halfway there. It was no use. Neither he nor Bud could shoulder the burden of Sunny's dead weight. Hard as it was, Bill finally roused her and forced Sunny to walk across the broken oyster shells to the sagging lean-to. Her eyes barely fluttered in recognition of being on dry land, but that was the extent of her celebration of being "rescued".

Old Bud had a light stroke a few years back, which left him with a slight limp and a stiff leg. The only work he'd been able to find since then was a low-paying job a a caretaker on this little island. He had always been a drinker, hence the near empty pint of gin still rattling around the bottom of the boat. Needless to say, he wasn't much help in shuttling the two survivors from the boat to the shack.

Once inside the cabin's cramped quarters, however, Bud at least tried to help Bill and Sunny into the bunks. They barely noticed the dust and mildew that rose and then resettled as their bodies found solace in the thin, flat mattresses they were offered.

The sunburns that scarred their backs made lying down painful, but the relief from their muscle-cramped legs made the burden at least bearable. As Bud turned around to leave, the two exhausted survivors begged him to take the money from the wallets Sunny had stuffed in the top of her dress.

The old man all too willingly obliged. Bill watched the gleam in his eye and worried, but even he had no time for his own skittishness. "Bud," he croaked the stained surface of the mattress feeling as soft and clean against his skin as if it was made of the finest silk, "there have to be people out looking for us. Our families, our friends, they must be terribly worried. You have to tell them where we are; you must tell them we're here. Please, please help us. Take our money, please, but don't forget about us. A few miles back from where you found us is where we split up form our friends. They must have drifted by now but please have somebody come back for us and send the others in that direction. You know the area well, tell them where to look. Bud, you're our only hope. Please man, do it for us!"

Halfway through his impassioned plea Bill noticed the glazed look in the old man's eyes, but chose to ignore it as he made one final request: "Bud, look at us. We're in bad shape. We need medicine, food, and water. Please don't leave us here stranded. We're begging you for help."

As a good faith gesture, Bud gave them all the water he had in the shack, which turned out to be a small amount. The two clutched their half-empty jars of lukewarm water as if they held claim to private pots of gold. As he licked his lips while counting the money in the wallets Sunny had offered, he promised to "hurry right back."

Mustering the very last of his rapidly-draining energy, Bill shouted after him, "Don't forget us, Bud. Tell them about the others and where they were last seen. My name is Bill, and this here lady is named Sunny. Bill and Sunny. Tell them to hurry. We need help as soon as we can get it."

The old man nodded his head, and then quickly shut the door behind him. As soon as he was out of sight he leaned against the outside of the cabin and finished counting the money he'd been given. It wasn't much, less than fifty bucks all told, but it would do...for now....

He quickly putt-putted the old boat the three miles to dry land. As he got closer to the shore, he ignored the most likely spots where rescuers might have gathered and instead veered straight to a dock area which was close to a small bar. He had time to spare, and needed to think about what to do with those two people back in his fishing shack. What where their names again? Escaping the heat, he went inside and thrilled to the cool, dark air that hung like a haze inside the small, crowded bar. Smoke filled the air, leaking in tendrils from the mouths of the busily-talking patrons.

At first their patter sounded like so much small talk, but as his first drink arrived-and this his second, and after his third, and then his fourth-he listened more closely to the buzz of people talking about the missing boaters. Splatters of conversation assailed his keen old ears like so many bugs against a wind-shield:

"...gone missing on Sunday..."

"...Over 54 hours without food or water, bobbing in that hot, hot sun..."

"...14 of them on the boat, how many of them are left, I've no idea..."

"...some of the nicest families you'd ever want to meet; I brought them sandwiches just this morning..."

Bud smiled smugly to himself, ordering another drink and keeping close track of what was left of *his* money. Slowly, as the afternoon progressed, he began to brag and drink, drink and brag.

"I know where some of "them" are," he said at last, raising his glass to the bar at large and smirking over its grease-smudged rim before tossing it back and ordering himself another, "Found 'em just over an hour ago. Or was it two? Seems the time escapes me, but sure enough they looked like the kind of folks the sun's baked and the ocean's pickled...."

The patrons listened to the old reprobate brag; he was enjoying the attention he was getting at the bar. For the first time since his stroke, he was actually feeling *very* important. He was also feeling no pain as he continued to tell the other patrons about the sunburned, nearly naked people he had found only a few miles from where they all sat.

Most of the bar patrons, who knew Bud well, ignored him. Others, who knew Bud by the local reputation that preceded him, ignored him even more soundly. However, someone that day finally believed him and called the authorities. Once the call had been made, the tenor of the bar shifted. What had been local scuttlebutt and gossip suddenly became serious…deadly serious. The bar closed in on Bud, and he who had so longed to be the center of attention quickly found the old adage to be all too true: be careful what you wish for.

It was official; the authorities were on their way. At that very moment Sheriff John Harris himself was cruising to the little bar, making record time in a squad car that had seen plenty of use in the last 48 hours or more. Meanwhile the bar became a hostile place, full of danger and the threat of implied violence lurking in those dark corners Bud had always loved so well. He was asked, repeatedly, where he'd found the survivors. What state they were in? How they had fared and what their names were, where they were and were they there anymore. After much posturing and arguing with his would-be interrogators, however, old Bud staunchly refused to say exactly where they were. Or for that matter, who they were…. Through blurry eyes and a tongue coated with too much gin he blurted, "You'll find out when the Sheriff does. Until then, you'll just have to wait." Those who were there that day noticed a gleam of satisfaction in his eye. Happily, it wouldn't stay there for long….

Sheriff John Harris pulled up to the ramshackle little bar in a haze of gravel and dust; he was standing in the parking lot before his car had even come to a complete stop. To say that Harris was furious would have been an understatement-he was absolutely, positively, literally irate. Practically tearing the door of the hinges, he held it open and pulled the old salt into the hot sunlight and fresh air, preferring to conduct his brief interrogation on his own turf, instead of standing in front of Bud's barstool. Bud was pretty drunk and staggering by then; the sudden change of climate wasn't helping matters any but Harris didn't care. Pulling himself up to his full height, the sheriff stuck his nose right in Bud's face and blurted, "Not only and I arresting you for public drunkenness, Bud, but if one of those survivors dies because you sat around some bar all afternoon drowning your sorrows, I'll bring you up on murder charges so fast it'll make your shrunken-in head spin. Now you're going to tell me where those survivors are and how to find them, and while I'm bringing them home safe you're going to pray they're alright. Start talking, Bud. NOW!"

Whether it was his volume or his promise of jail, Sheriff Harris' threats seemed to do the trick. "There's two of 'em, see," Bud suddenly "recalled" through his drunken haze. He tried holding up two fingers for emphasis but needed all the support he could get so quickly returned both hands to the weathered railing of the bar's dilapidated front porch. He burped loudly before continuing his ramshackle story: "They told me their names but I don't remember quite rightly what they is now, Sunshine or something. They're at the old fishing cabin I watch off Cedar Key. You know the one, out there in the flats? Laid'em up in the bunks there and they was fine when I left'em. Had plenty of water for'em, too. You should be thankin' me, Sheriff, 'stead of arresting me. I should get some kind of reward, don'tcha think?"

The look on Harris' face stopped that line of reasoning dead in its tracks. "Go on," Harris seethed. "I'm listening."

Bud swallowed and finished his tale: "They said there was four or five more of them floating east off the Key, my bet was they were trying to head for shore. Who knows, Sheriff? They might have even made it by now. Follow the coast down there and you'll run into 'em, I reckon."

The sheriff was beside himself and, shaking his head, lamented, "All this wasted time." Using his car radio he immediately alerted the searchers of the latest news and began to gather men in boats for the rescue. The men who had been lingering in the doorway listening to Bud and Harris' conversation leapt to the rescue, untying their boats and fighting over who might have the honor of taking Harris to the ramshackle shack off Cedar Key.

As Harris and his posse headed out to rescue the unknown survivors the families at Yankeetown were duly alerted to come to Cedar Key. According to the Sheriff, there were "possible survivors."

"Thank God!" came a cry at the dock as Harris' men informed the families of the survivors. "Survivors have been found!" they continued, instructing the families, "We are on our way to pick them up. Go to Cedar Key dock.

It was a 35 minutes trip to reach the lonely fishing shack and back to the dock, and it would almost be sunset before they got Bill and Sunny back to land. *That was*, Harris thought, *if they were still alive*. The local authorities joined up with the Marion County Sheriff's Department to aid in the recovery of victims. Several motor boats got under way immediately, quickly joining the contingent as one and all sped straight to Cedar Key.

Back at the island, Bill was starting to worry. Buoyed by the rest and the water, what little of it Bud had left them, he found himself ignoring his own needs and thinking of the other survivors instead. As a sudden realization washed over him he leaned over the edge of his bunk and whispered to Sunny, "I think Buck and the others may have gotten turned around and headed in the wrong direction."

Sunny did her best to respond, but her fluttering eyes and trembling body did little to reassure Bill that time was not, in fact, running out for her. He laid back in his bunk, the wooden slats beneath his frame squeaking in protest as he silently prayed that the rescuers would find the others in time.

Out on the open water setting a course straight for Cedar Key, two rescue boats sped across the waves toward the salt flats, led by Chief Sheriff Deputy Matt McGuire himself. One of the boats sighted...something...floating in the water.

A rescuer named Rusty sounded off the discovery. "Got something out there, get close and let me have a look." Chief McGuire slowed the boat by way of a response, watching as Rusty rushed to the side of the boat. All of the rescuers feared the worst, and as they slowed to cruising speed and approached the bobbing figure, their worst fears were realized: it was a body in a life jacket. "Hey, Matt," Rusty cried out, "What do I do?? It's a dead body!"

The lifeless woman was clearly dead, her skin pale and waxy and covered with the infinitesimal creatures that had plagued all of the survivors during their days-long ordeal. There was no time to feel for a pulse or drag her onboard. Chief McGuire closed his eyes, said a silent prayer, shook his head, and answered from the front of the boat, "Rusty, go ahead and tie a couple of our empty gas cans on, and let's go look for some that are alive, they need us more that this poor soul." That done, the rescuers continued on.

Bill and Sunny were drifting in and out of consciousness by the time Sheriff John Harris kicked open the door of the little fishing shack. Dusk was close and his flashlight beam caught Bill's near naked torso in its high-powered shaft of light. He never thought he'd be so happy to see another grown man in his altogether as he was at that very moment!

Here were two of the people he'd been searching for over the last two days. He hadn't slept; he knew they hadn't either. Nor had their families, their friends, or a legion of volunteer rescuers just wanting to lend a helping hand. With all this in mind, he tried to keep his emotions in check as he directed his men to cover the two survivors-carefully-and begin hydrating them with the water they'd brought along for that very purpose.

Bill and Sunny were rousted gently from their bunks and carried by several men to Harris' own boat. McGuire had just caught up with the other rescuers at the suddenly crowded area on the tiny island.

It was a decidedly subdued scene on the dock as the two weary survivors were loaded onto the boat and made to feel comfortable. Bill was resolute in directing the rescuers to their fellow survivors. Sunny helped, as well, but despite the extra water and gentle treatment she was still fading in and out. Sheriff Harris tried to reassure them both that boats were speeding toward the area to look for the survivors. Bill smiled uncertainly while Sunny nodded as if she hadn't heard. Harris looked at them both then signaled to his captain.

Let's move it! It was time for these two survivors to get medical attention…

In the hubbub of the rescue the body floating in the ocean was almost, but not completely, forgotten. Two rescue boats went back to retrieve the woman's body, led by Matt McGuire. Even with their leader at the helm, though, the rescuers on board were far from prepared for what they found. When they got there two large sharks were already feeding on the corpse, the water a frothing mass of fins and blood as they interrupted feeding time. Thinking quickly, the men used paddles to strike the sleek, gray skin of the sharks and, when that didn't work, they tossed in a heavy anchor to drive the sharks away. Unfortunately, the damage had already been done: all that was left of the once vibrant woman was her face and torso. It was a grisly sight, and to a man the crews of both boats rushed to the sides to throw up. Grim work lay ahead as Deputy McGuire and Rusty reached over to lift what was left of the body from the ocean and secured it in the back of the boat. Chief McGuire knew who the woman was as soon as he saw her long red hair. McGuire said with choked emotion, "Oh dear Lord, I know this woman. I *know* her. It's Lacey Ross. Lex's wife. My wife, Krysta and I buy our shoes from their shoe store. They both go to my church. If this happened to Lacey, what on earth has happened to Lex????"

CHAPTER 22

Help is on the Way

Yankeetown dock was swollen with friends, relatives, rescuers, firemen, the city council, and anyone and everyone who knew-or even thought they knew-one of the survivors. The old boards of the already sagging dock stretched nearly to the water with the weight of them all, and with the word that survivors had been found the desperate crowd rushed the poor deputy who had been summoned.

Now the car radio in the poor rookie's trembling right hand squawked to life again. The garbled transmission bleating into the night was almost indecipherable, except for one word: "Sunny."

"Sunny is alive!" yelled the deputy, the relieved look on his face all but illuminating the darkness that was enveloping the crowd. "Sunny is alive!" The crowd literally erupted. Shouts of joy filled the night air as they swarmed the young man; the first to bring them relief in nearly three days.

There would be little time for celebration. Despite his jubilation the deputy silenced the surrounding mob with a sharp look and an impatient wave of his hand. He listened closely to the instructions Sheriff Harris was giving him before finally shouting, "Everyone is to go to Cedar Key! That's where they're bringing them. Go to Cedar Key."

As cheers drowned out the last of his statement and motors sprang to life in a mechanical chorus, the officer turned to Sunny's mother and asked the elated woman to accompany him on the ride. It seemed like the only proper thing to do, and the poor woman seemed thunderstruck at the offer.

In the rush to the narrow parking lot the two were quickly joined by several tired and relieved relatives, who loaded up in the patrol car, arms and leg akimbo, looking much like the clown car at the circus. The description fit: like smiling clowns, they were all so happy and relieved, imagining that the worst of the worry, grief, and frustration was almost over.

Thereafter, a mad dash ensued. Yankeetown, once a thriving hub of activity, quickly became more like a ghost town. Captains took to their boats, deputies to their squad cars, and the rest of the relatives forced themselves to let the professionals lead the way as they followed in impromptu carpools that rattled and rolled through the night. It was an unlikely- and uncertain-caravan. As the drove, the families were crying, laughing, and thanking God, all at the same time.

Sadly, they did not yet know that all had not been found….

The convoy roared through the night, making the 48 mile trip from Yankeetown to Cedar Key in record time. With sirens ablaze and the streets deserted, they arrived en masse, family members and law enforcement personnel alike streaming from the cars like ants in an ant hill.

Soon after they arrived at Cedar Key, seven boats converged on the already crowded dock. The first two had Sunny and Bill on board. Seeing the dazed and seared survivors sent an electric shock through everyone assembled; hands flew to faces as necks craned for a better sight of the bedraggled survivors.

Tears of relief and joy streamed down male and female faces alike; everyone was so relieved that the emotions literally poured out of them, unbidden. All the family members and rescuers were certain that the rest of the boats contained all 14 of the survivors. The anxious mothers peered into the other boats, calling out the names of their missing loved ones. It was a one-sided serenade, for time after time no loved one answered their pained, anguished cries of hope mixed with growing despair.

Lynn Morgan and Mabel Jennings were in the forefront. They called out their girls' names, again and again, hoping for some kind of reply, no matter how weak or feeble. No one answered. Delirious by now and unable to respond to the cries of their loved ones, Bill and Sunny were placed in an awaiting ambulance where I.V. fluids were started to re-hydrate the pair, who were lucky to be alive. Sheriff Harris hovered around the back of the ambulance, the relief on his face masked by concern and impatience over the fate of the other survivors. He had lost precious time thanks to the drunk old caretaker's foolishness. How much more time could he spend waiting around for Bill and Sunny to come to?

The ambulance crew was aware of his predicament; they worked quickly to make sure the two survivors were revived as quickly and safely as possible. At last, the flicker of life returned to their eyes and the crew signaled the Sheriff that he could begin his questions. Finally, Sheriff Harris asked the question that all were waiting to hear answered. Now that the survivors had been given some fluids, they were able to speak a little, stammering and coughing around their swollen tongues as they tried to answer the stern-looking Sheriff. He looked at the two survivors and asked what happened to the boat, "Where are the others?" In reply, Sunny merely rolled her head from side to side, remembering the horror of the last few days; the shock of it rendered her speechless.

For his part, Bill was torn between answering for her and whispering reassurances to her. Meanwhile, Sheriff Harris made room for several of the family members, who'd been eavesdropping over his shoulder the whole time.

Mabel leaned around the sheriff and asked, "Honey, where is your sister?" The answer caused the small lady to drop to her knees, where she screamed, "Jesus, Lord, God, NOOOOO!!!!" The sound of a mother's grief chilled the crowd. Sunny's answer, "We separated…we may be the only ones who made it." Whispered first from Sheriff Harris to his deputies and then from family member to family member, rocketed through the crowd like a living thing. One by one, the relatives heard the awful news, and promptly joined each other in screaming, moaning, and crying.

This shockwave rippled through the crowd and back; the ambulance was it's epicenter. Disbelief, tempered with doubt, met the grim news. Some were certain they'd misheard; others believed it at face value. Many relatives rushed to the ambulance, their bodies crushing against each other as they surged forward, needing more news, desperate for information. Hoping. Hoping. They wanted to hear anything that might give them some hope.

Bill, able to speak for the first time, stuttered uncharacteristically as he admitted, "W-w-we last saw the five others this m-m-morning around d-daylight. They headed away from us to find an island. Buck was leading Sam, Analee, Kate, and Lacey. We haven't seen them since."

A living breathing thing now, the crowd gasped in unison; it was the first time they'd heard a glimmer of hope since Sunny spoke. Bill shook his head, ignoring the crowd, picturing the scene, and croaked sadly, "We can only hope they made it."

Sheriff Harris forced his way through the crowd, barking orders into his walkie-talkie as he took giant strides back toward the dock. He was on the water, leading a fresh group of rescuers out into the night, even before Bill had spoken the last words and rested his head back on his pillow.

Amazingly, there was still hope....

CHAPTER 23

More Survivors

In the water four passengerssurvivors floated, near death. Three wore vests, one did not. Through the listless paddling of the fading human beings, the dolphins remained vigilant, circling the group, darting in front of and behind them, offering comfort in their presence, as well as defense. As if sensing the last, they were deathly quiet; their clickety-clackety chatter long since silenced by the pall of hopelessness that has descended upon the close cluster of floating, bobbing survivors.

The dolphins' vigil is not without precedent; alert sharks circle the perimeter, their dorsal fins a constant companion to both human and dolphin alike. It is an ongoing standoff, and were the dolphins to leave the area, the sharks would most certainly have a field day feasting on the unprotected humans.

As a group, the four survivors, almost drowned, were a pitiful sight. They were literally cooked by the sun and dried out by the heat; their skin was a pulsating purple, almost every square inch above the water's surface blistered and boiled. Flakes of dried salt from the briny seawater dusted their necks and the bottoms of their ears, literally salting their wounds. They had taken about all they could stand, but still had a determined hope to reach land.

By that point, it was about all they had left....

Buck eyed the rag-tag crew from beneath hooded lids. It hurt to open his eyes any further; the skin of his face swollen and cracked. One by one, he took stock of the survivors, as he'd been doing every hour since splitting up from Bill and Sunny that afternoon. His captain might have been gone, half his "party" was dead, as well, but he still felt responsible for the safety of the rest of his passengers and, as long as there was air in his lungs and his head was above water, he would continue.

It was not just a sense of duty that found him eyeing his charges, but a deep-seated sense of responsibility. After all, he had been the one to suggest that a spit of land was out there, somewhere, waiting for them to find it. So far, the pursuit had been in vain; the small island he'd thought was so close never materialized. He wondered, from time to time, how Bill and Sunny had fared, and if in fact his plan to split up had been little more than a fool's errand.

He shook his head consciously, effectively erasing the thought. If there was one thing he'd learned from the ordeal it was not to look back with regret, but forward with purpose. "Focus," he told himself. "Assess the survivors. Do what needs to be done."

Sam, he knew, was unconscious, maybe even dead. His head lolled from side to side like a child's rag doll, limp and lifeless; he hadn't opened his eyes in hours now. His life jacket, like the others, was waterlogged and of little use. Buck knew they didn't have long before the already pitiful jackets lost whatever buoyancy they still had left.

By then, he had given up hope of lasting through the night. He knew if they weren't rescued soon, none of them would be alive come morning. Even if the life jackets survived, Buck knew their frail human bodies would not. Even Buck, a hale and hearty man of the sea, felt so close to death he could almost taste it; he couldn't imagine how the others had lasted this long.

Buck thought of Lacey; he knew they lost her hours earlier. Once she'd made the decision to follow Bill and Sunny, he knew she'd made her choice. Perhaps it was better that way.

At least she could join her husband now, though the thought brought him little peace. It seemed unnatural to choose death over life, but he knew delirium affects everyone differently. Some saw their loved ones, beckoning to them from beneath the ocean's depths. Others saw mirages-land where there was none, pure water where only saltwater remained. Perhaps she'd thought Bill and Sunny were closer than they actually were; maybe she thought she'd do it better on her own. Either way, he didn't expect to see her again....

Analee looked resolute, but even her youth and vitality could not stave off the inevitable effects of surviving on the open sea for over 56 hours. She was dehydrated, way past hunger, and slipping fast. It pained Buck to see hope drained from the beautiful young girl's face.

How long, he wondered, *had it been since she last smiled?*

Kate was even worse. She was slightly better than Sam, but far worse off than either Buck or Analee, who were also fading fast. He'd seen the look of impending death one too many times by now. Sadly, he recognized it on Kate's pale, gaunt face. If only there was something, *anything*, he could do....

Buck finished assessing the survivors, and then asked them to form a circle and hold onto one another. "Closer," he urged, eyeing the dolphins as they circled endlessly, and then the sharks just beyond their reach. "Closer"

As they moved listlessly toward him, he was blunt in reasoning. If anyone else dies," he croaked, "at least they will not die alone. I don't want to lose anyone else the way we lost Lacey. We're in this together now, folks, and I'm not going to let another one of you go off on your own again. Whatever happens to one of us happens to all of us. Got that?" Grim faces, all nodding except for Sam, met his declaration. They pulled up to each other, huddling very close, so weak, barely able to even whisper a grunt of gratitude, let alone an encouraging word. Despite her own worsening condition, Analee was helping Buck keep Kate's head above water. It was a tireless perhaps futile task; she wondered how long she could keep it up. They were so tired, it was almost impossible for them to help each other any longer. Discomfort was a long forgotten memory, pain a constant companion. Still, survival was all that mattered.

They knew that to quit on each other now meant to give up on life itself.

"Please help me, Lord," Analee cried suddenly, shocking those around her. "I don't know how much more I can take."

"Kate," she whispered solemnly, eager to give the dying woman some hope for the future. She chose her words carefully, using strong language and the absolute certainty of their rescue, though she wasn't sure of herself, as she said, "When this is over, I want you to come and stay with me and Momma. We will help you raise your baby."

Buck nodded his assent, fearing she might never get the chance to make good on her generous promise. The lapping of water, so familiar, so torturous, lulled them into submission as they grimly faced more time on the open sea.

Buck could not help but wonder how long....

Meanwhile, a ragtag fleet of rescuers followed in the wake of a Coast Guard cutter. It was a desperate search, for as the afternoon dwindled evening was quickly falling. On board the cutter, alert Coast Guardsmen knew they had only limited time to work. It was growing dark quickly, and they knew if they didn't find the survivors in the next few passes with the searchlight, it would soon be too dark to see them. As the hopeful seamen shined their light on the water, at last one of the Coast Guardsmen saw a glimmer of something in the light of the last pass and called out, "My GOD it's them!"

In the distance, a sound got the survivors' attention. *Could it be?* Buck wondered, shaking his head even as he asked. *It couldn't be, could it?*

It grew louder and more certain.

"Dear God," Buck cried, "I think someone's found us! It's the Coast Guard!" Thank God.

The sea swelled with the presence of several rescue boats, their skippers careful not to flood the survivors in their wake. Even so, waves from their approach buffeted the pitiful group, splashing onto their faces making them wince in pain. For once, they didn't mind the intrusion! Buck watched, almost beyond belief as uniformed men leapt into the open sea to pull them from the water that had been their home for nearly three days now.

They were too tired for jubilation, too weary to be more thankful. They knew only that they were going home, the buoyancy of their rescue tempered by the loss of the others.

Even as the survivors were being pulled from the sea, Buck could not help but notice Sam's lifeless body. Would he make it? Buck doubted it. Meanwhile, the coast guardsmen radioed the news back to shore, their message as short as it was full of impact: "There are three more survivors."

Buck was right: Sam did not make it, nor did Lacey.

As Analee was hoisted aboard to waiting hands a young guardsman squatted down as he laid her on deck to cut off her floatation device. It was the same alert young man who had spotted the glimmer from her lifejacket. Now he noticed that the source was, in fact, Sam's pin. She looked a wreck, but her eyes were alert and so he cleared his throat and felt urged to explain, "My name is Bobby. We were about to give up until we saw our light reflect off something."

Perhaps sensing the grief in her heart, the young coastguardsmen continued, "Ma'am, thank God we found you…most of the town has been praying at the Yankeetown dock ever since we learned y'all were missing. Thank God, we spotted you. Thank you, Jesus." Analee's eyes fluttered at the news, and though she could not reply, a nod from her was thanks enough.

As they lay Sam beside her on the deck, she leaned over and took his cold hand in hers, touched her lips to his and whispered, "We are home, Sam…Goodbye dearest one."

Even as they were being pulled onboard, expertly trained Coast Guard sharpshooters were busy firing at the sharks that had been circling in the immediate area. One by one the predators were either killed or driven away.

The ocean frothed with their blood and whipped tails, but it mattered little anymore; the survivors were safe aboard the Coast Guard boats.

The dolphins' job was done, and at last they swam away to do whatever dolphins do when they aren't protecting shipwrecked humans in the sea. The survivors, instantly swept up into the expert care of the capable Coast Guard medics, neither noticed nor were able to thank their constant companions, their loyal guardians. Perhaps their survival was thanks enough for the faithful mammals....

CHAPTER 24

Ocala

Ocala's reaction to the unprecedented maritime tragedy was immediate and swift. On Friday, July 5, most of the stores in Ocala remained closed. Flags flew at half mast from all of the Marion County offices, as well as banks, and even the Post Office; a first, except during wartime.

Ocala became a ghost town, and even those who were on the streets for one reason or another walked slowly, solemnly, as if afraid to disrespect the memory of those brave souls who had lost their lives at sea.

Black wreaths hung from Green's drugstore, the Car dealership, the barbershop, the now closed Ocala Hardware Store, and the Family Shoe Shop. At the Memorial Service for those lost in this tragedy, the church was so crowded that they opened all the doors so people could stand outside and hear the service. To say there was not a dry eye in the house would have been the pinnacle of understatement. More likely, there wasn't a dry eye in all of Ocala that day.

On Friday, at noon, the town whistle blew one long and lonely blast for each victim, nine long blasts.

On the radio, Ocala Mayor John Marshall Green thanked all the rescuers for their valiant efforts. He especially thanked the Highway Patrol, and the Sheriff's department, in particular, Sheriff Harris and his deputies for all the hours they put in to bring the citizens back home. He sent a letter to the Coast Guard for their tireless efforts.

He also sent letter of appreciation to the Yankeetown residents who played such a key role assisting the relatives at the dock. A letter also went to the

Mayor of Cedar Key, thanking the residents of his small town for their part in the rescue of the boaters.

The rescue had truly been a joint effort, and in the days to come the Mayor would continually be confronted with fresh faces he'd forgotten to thank. Again and again he would recall how this person had brought a plate of sandwiches to Yankeetown docks, or stopped in with a pie to City Hall. So many had given so generously of their time; thanklessly, wordlessly, without a second thought.

It would take him years to thank them all...

Sheriff Harris received his thanks with a restive grin, his first—and last—of the day. He alone had been present from the first family member's call to the last of their loved one's funerals. He had watched Yankeetown dock swell with hope, and then drain with fear at the prospect that not all of the survivors had, in fact survived.

That day found him pacing his office, fielding calls from this reporter or that, still wearing his dress uniform, having neglected to take it off after the memorial service. The Mayor had given him the rest of the day off, urging him to go home and get some rest, but though he'd driven off in that direction after the service he'd promptly turned around in his own driveway and the connectedness of his office.

Outside his closed door the phones rang and officers walked around, dazed, with black band strapped around their arms in remembrance of the dead. It was a rare, if fitting, tribute to the civilians who had faced their deaths with the bravery and resoluteness of those charged to protect and serve.

Harris felt it was the least his men could do...

In the stale vacuum left behind by the massive and all-encompassing rescue effort, Harris suddenly found himself with little to do. There were various forms to fill out, and the requisite paperwork to shuffle, but he quickly found himself sitting at his desk unable to form a coherent sentence, tired, he was so tired.

As the afternoon wore on he became less and less efficient. His door remained shut, his secretary screening his calls and barring concerned deputies and colleagues from entering. At last, Sheriff Harris slumped onto his desk, the sleep that had long been denied him overtaking him as swiftly and powerfully, he had kept it at bay for nearly three straight days.

Like so many in Ocala that day, sleep became his only relief...

Epilogue

Life moved on in the wake of the tragedy. Ocala shops opened their doors, and Yankeetown dock once again emptied bright and early each morning as its remaining captains headed out to sea to make their living.

Even those who had been most deeply affected by the senseless disaster, the survivors themselves, moved on. Literally: After a few days in the hospital, the small group of survivors was finally released home to their families.

In a few days the brave barber known as Bill was back in his shop giving haircuts and shaving his customers; it was as if he'd never left. Folks marveled at his strength and resilience, but to Bill it seem only logical that he should look forward, and not backward. Besides, he could barely stand the emptiness of his home without his beloved wife, Lois.

In his cold, empty bed or staring at his wife's empty chair and the dinner table, he was lost, bereft, helpless. At least at work, among his faithful customers and listening to the reassuring sounds of his snipping shears, he was finally at peace.

He was doing the best he could for his now motherless children. Lois's mom stayed to help with the kids, and together they formed an unlikely bond that would never be broken. In a time of intense need and nearly bottomless despair, she and Bill helped each other grieve through this painful period.

The beautiful young swimmer from Silver Springs stayed true to her word: Analee *did* take Kate home with her. In fact, Kate was welcomed with open arms by the entire Morgan family. Arms that opened it seemed, in more ways than one: Analee's older brother, David actually fell in love with Kate; a year after her baby was born she and David were married.

Not all of the survivors were so lucky. Sunny found life after the tragedy particularly difficult. She had lost so much, and so many, out on that open sea. The pain was unbearable, intense, and seemingly without limit.

She was traumatized by her husband's death, as well as her sister, Ginny's, and brother-in-law, Pete's demise. Not only had she lost the man she'd loved so dearly, but the two "Love birds' were gone as well. The birds had been forgotten; a look into the cage that housed the beautiful love birds revealed that Pete and Petey were dead. They were found lying side by side on the bottom of the cage.

About seven months after the incident, Sunny met a young Coast Guardsman name Tom. They fell in love and were married. Sadly, however, her nightmares never ended; sometimes she had terrifying flashbacks. Pete's death, in particular, plagued her to no end. For years she remembered his ghostly, haunting voice as he begged her, over and over for "…a Cooo-ca, Cooo-la, a Cooo-ca, Cooo-la."

She had survived it seemed, but Pete's ghost remained behind to haunt her…

As for Bud, Sunny and Bill's unlikely rescuer, he was eventually released from police custody and returned to his old ways. Although the Sheriff was eager to charge him criminally, the survivors were so grateful for his "help" that they went to bat for him, saving him from the jail time such a charge would have most certainly entailed.

Very few thought of Bud as a hero.

The fishing guide, Buck, returned home to his loving Betty Jo and their happy family. He often liked to look at them and realize just how lucky he was to have survived his tragedy at sea.

Not a day went by, however, that he didn't reflect at some point to pay homage to his dear captain, L.B. Wilson. Like all the survivors, his guilt over living where others close to him had perished remained. The five who had survived their ordeal had formed an indelible bond as they bobbed endlessly on the open sea; they were forever changed from the ordeal, and none of them emerged unscathed.

They moved on, lived life, married, had kids, ate dinner, and took naps. They celebrated holidays, birthdays, anniversaries, and new years. They laughed, cried, prayed, walked, and looked just like "normal" people. Normal people, however, they were not. As survivors, they lived their lives with a singular purpose: to live every day as if it might be their last.

In the end, *that* was the survivor's legacy…

Mable Jennings continued to work at the Drug Store. The next year there was again a family picnic. Again the pallets went down for small children to nap; again Mable handed out glass jars for fire flies. The happiness felt there had changed forever. Fred & Dolores the couple who declined the invitation for the fishing trip gave birth to a son—Terry, and later another son, Larry—Anne had a sixth child, a girl they named Virginia. Life goes on. People are missed.

978-0-595-40182-6
0-595-40182-1

Printed in the United States
74164LV00004B/1-48